The

Lower Case

Volume 4 of the

Case Books of Octavius Bear

Harry DeMaio

"Alternative Universe Mysteries for Adult Animal Lovers"

Paperback ISBN 978-1-78092-951-4
ePub ISBN 978-1-78092-952-1
PDF ISBN 978-1-78092-953-8

Published in the UK by MX Publishing
335 Princess Park Manor, Royal Drive,
London, N11 3GX
www.mxpublishing.co.uk

Dedicated to GTP

A Most Extraordinary Bear

and

to the Memory of Bob Gibson

A Most Extraordinary Artist

Acknowledgements

These books have evolved over a long period of time and under a wide range of influences and circumstances. I am indebted to many people for helping to bring Octavius and his cohorts to the printed page. Thanks most especially to my wife, Virginia, for her insights and clever suggestions as well as her unfailing enthusiasm for the project and patience with its author. To my sons, Mark and Andrew and their spouses, Cindy and Lorraine, for helping make these tomes more readable and audience friendly. To (Madame) Cathy Hartnett, cheerleader-extraordinaire for her eagerness to see this alternate universe take form. To Jack Magan, Rick Talerico, Dan Andriacco, Amy Thomas and Zohreh Zand for their assistance and support.

Kudos to Jim Effler, Bob Gibson and Brian Belanger for their illustrations and covers. Thanks, of course, to Steve Emecz and MX Publishing for giving Octavius et al. a great home.

If, in spite of all this help, some errors or inconsistencies have crept through, the buck stops here. Needless to say, all of the characters, situations, and narratives are fictional.

The Development of Civilization Volume 4 Part 1

Our Origins

(From "An Introduction to Faunapology" by Octavius Bear Ph.D.)

About 100,000 years ago, according to scientific experts, a colossal solar flare blasted out from our Sun, creating gigantic magnetic storms here on Earth. These highly charged electrical tempests caused startling physical and psychological imbalances in the then population of our world. The complete nervous systems of some species were totally destroyed. For example, "Homo Sapiens" lost all mental and motor capabilities and rapidly became extinct. Less developed species exposed to the radiation were affected differently. Four-footed and finned mammals, birds and reptiles suddenly found themselves capable of complex thought, enhanced emotions, self-awareness, social consciousness and the ability to communicate, sometimes orally, sometimes telepathically, often both. Both speech production and speech perception slowly progressed with the evolution of tongues, lips, vocal cords and enhanced ear to brain connections. Many species developed opposable digits, fingers or claws, further accelerating civilized progress. Some others (most fish and underground dwellers) were shielded from the radiation and remained only as sentient as they were before the blast. This event is referred to as **The Big Shock**. It remains under intensive study.

The Players in Volume 4

Octavius Bear – Mega sized Kodiak; Narcoleptic war hero; Consulting Detective; Scientist; Inventor; Seeker of Justice; Mega-billionaire owner of Universal Ursine Industries; Gourmet/gourmand; Somewhat sedentary and grouchy just on general principles.

Mauritius (Maury) Meerkat – Narrator; Assistant to Octavius; Theatrical Agent; African *émigré* with a French-Dutch background; clever with a shady history.

Bearoness Belinda Béarnaise Bruin Bear *(nee Black)* – Gorgeous polar superstar, with the Aquashow, "Some Like It Cold." Now wife of Octavius; Very rich widow of Bearon Byron Bruin living in Bearmoral Castle in the Shetlands; Owner-pilot of the last flying Concorde SST.

Bearyl and Bearnice Blanc – Belinda's stunning twin polar sidekicks; Actress and singer, respectively; Co-pilot and flight engineer of Belinda's SST.

Leperello - (Lepi) - Himalayan Snow Leopard and singing partner of Bearnice Blanc.

Madame Honoria Heifer – Cow – Infuriating voice coach for Bearnice and Lepi.

Otto the Magnificent – AKA Hairy Otter - An absolutely terrible illusionist magician, Otto the Magnificent escaped the claws of the evil genius Imperius Drake, but not before he developed some amazing powers courtesy of Imperius' genetic alterations.

Frau Schuylkill – Octavius' beautiful Swiss she-wolf housekeeper/cook/pilot/ security officer with many other mysterious and military talents. She rescued Octavius from his dive off the Breakurbach Falls while he was struggling with his nemesis, Imperius Drake.

Wyatt Where – Another wolf. Former military intelligence officer who had retired to a security post at the Bank of Lake Michigan in Chicago and then quit to join Octavius.

Howard Watt – Porcupine. High tech security authority who also left the Bank with Wyatt Where to join Octavius. A laser and particle beam accelerator expert.

L. Condor – Andean Condor cyber-net genius with a 12-foot wingspan.

Forrest F. Fox –Winnipeg Based Criminal Lawyer.

Chita – AKA Madame Catherine Catt - Beautiful, fascinating, clever, sexy, immoral and highly independent feline who among other things, is the publisher and editor in chief of *PURR* and *SOW* magazines.

Cyd – Chita's probably fictitious twin sister.

Imperius Drake – "Moriarty with wings." Arch-villain, leader of the Black Quack gang; brilliant but loony duck who has developed a serum to make the animal kingdom his slaves;

Superintendent Rowan Caballus of the Royal Canadian Unmounted Police (RCUP) – Horse

Sergeant Preston RCUP – Officious and none too bright dog.

Kitty and Maxie – Canada Lynx – Proprietors of Kitty's Kozy Korner – a Winnipeg neighborhood bar

The Staff at CWP – TV

> **Wally Wapiti** – Station Manager
>
> **Beatrice Beaver** – Features Reporter and Anchor
>
> **Felicia Foxx** – Assistant to Beatrice Beaver
>
> **Morley Moose** – News Anchor
>
> **Grigor Gregory** – Special Events Manager – a Grizzly Bear

The Staff at the Winnipeg Opera

> **Dr. Woodrow Wolverine** – Opera Director
>
> **Godfrey Gander** – Associate Director
>
> **Herr Professor Doktor Dieter von Tripp** – Red Stag – Musical Director

Hartley Hare –Orchestra Leader

Giselle – Mountain Goat – Pianist

Bartholomew Badger – Security Officer

Marty – Communications Manager – Stone Marten

Viveca Vixen – Assistant to the Opera Director

Superintendent Nigel Wardlaw of Shetland Yard – Bearded Collie –The Scottish Police.

Fetlock Holmes – The Great Horse Detective and sometime associate of Octavius Bear.

Doctor "Odd" Vark – Aardvark – Chief Geneticist at Universal Ursine Industries.

Doctor Chiti BingBang – Orangutan – Chief Physician at Universal Ursine Industries.

Locations in Volume 4

Winnipeg, Churchill and Manitoba, Canada; Cincinnati, Ohio; Bearmoral Castle, Unst and Baltasound in the Shetlands; Edinbeargh, Scotland

Also from Harry DeMaio

The Open and Shut Case

The Case of the Spotted Band

The Case of Scotch

Prologue

Monday Morning - Winnipeg, Manitoba

This weather is getting quite old.
I hate the Canadian cold.
But it's simply my luck
To be frozen and stuck
Until my wild "tail" is all told.

The jet stair rolled up to the door with the traditional thumps and bumps. One of the polar twins, Bearyl or Bearnice, pulled switches, turned handles and swung open the pressure door of the Flying Aquabear, the lone surviving, airworthy Concorde SST, pride of Octavius' wife, Bearoness Belinda Béarnaise Bruin Bear *(nee Black.) (The lady has been around.)* I had half risen from my grossly oversized ursine-tailored seat and was smacked in the face with a true Canadian welcome – blustery Arctic air. Welcome to Manitoba!

For someone who has spent most of his early life in holes and tunnels in the sun-baked Kalahari Desert, I seem doomed to finish out my existence in the most frigid climes of the universe. I'm a Meerkat. My name is Maury (Mauritius) Meerkat, wily detective, high powered talent agent, unprepossessing utility infielder, lovable friend to millions and most of all, indispensable chancellor to the sovereign, Octavius Bear. He's not really regal. He just acts that way.

Pardon my chattering teeth, but we have just disembarked in Winnipeg, Canada from the Shetland Islands. Out of the refrigerator and into cryogenics.

Unlike my ursine boss and his wolf companions who will be joining us in a day or so and also unlike our current entourage, the twin polar bears and Leperello, a Himalayan Snow leopard, I wasn't built to withstand cold...especially winter Canadian cold. There is one other animal on board, Honoria Heifer, a Scottish cow and vocal coach who is on the tour with us. She was lowing plaintively in her most dramatic mezzo soprano about the temperature, wind, bleak atmosphere and the entire experience of air travel. In an extravagantly outfitted Concorde, no less! Fortunately, although it was impossible to tune her out, we had all learned to ignore her. That may not be so easy as the week wears on.

But first, a little more background. Octavius Bear, my aforementioned employer, first rate consulting detective, mutual confidant and classic pain in the tail is, among his many talents and accomplishments, a brilliant, self-taught practitioner in the wide ranging fields of biology, physics, ursinology, voodoo, teleology, chemistry, apiculture and oenology. A self-made megabillionaire, he is also a first rate electrical, electronic, structural, marine, aeronautical, civil, mechanical and chemical engineer.

Early in his career, he developed a cure for the annoying need for bears to hibernate, allowing him to dedicate himself year-round to his businesses, personal avocations and especially his primary vocation – the protection and betterment of all "animal-kind." Unfortunately, unknown (or more likely, unaccepted) by him to this day, the cure has a side effect. The Great Bear falls off into periodic and usually poorly timed, narcoleptic sleep that can last from a few seconds to upwards of an hour. Once he wakes up again, he blithely carries on as if nothing had happened.

He is currently back in the Bear's Lair near Cincinnati with the rest of his team. He shuttles between Ohio and Belinda's opulent castle in the Shetlands. It is common knowledge that bears like to burrow, and Octavius does everything in grand style. His labs, shops, and launch facilities are underground and about twenty times larger than his above-ground mansion that by itself would give Buckingham Palace a run for it. He bought the mansion in the last stages of decay from an Ohio River steamboat captain who was down in his luck, and then totally gutted and restructured the interior to fit the needs of a sedentary but nine foot tall *(standing erect)* 1,400 pound Kodiak tycoon.

The only things that suggest there may be more to the property than meets the eye are the missile silo and launch pad, disguised as an oriental pagoda and the Romanesque hangar where the Bear keeps his highly customized stealth C-5A Galaxy, "*Ursa Major*" and several other airplanes. The aircraft, missile, missile silo, and control center, gifts from the government, were hangovers from the Great Inter-Species War, and Octavius decided to restore the systems and make them operational. As far as I know, he has never fired them in anger. A little pique perhaps, but not anger.

The huge plane, a gift from the Air Force after one of Octavius' secret but highly successful missions on their behalf is, in fact, a flying headquarters, lab and if necessary, weapons platform. The runway is cleverly disguised as an Interstate By-Pass that has been under construction for the past eight years.

Complete with orange marker barrels, warning signs, and fake bulldozers, the runway has fooled the local populace and successive governments into believing it is just leisurely highway construction as usual.

Right now, his primary concern is for his spouse, Bearoness Belinda Béarnaise, who to the surprise of all, recently discovered she was pregnant and immediately fell off into deep hibernation. *(Female polar bears hibernate only during pregnancy.)* Anyway, Octavius is committed to join us here in Winnipeg as Bearnice and Lepi embark on their major singing tour. They had been a sensation in their debut performance in Edinbeargh and as their agent, I developed a multi-city tour for them using the money and influence of the Bearoness and Octavius. Since Bearnice got her start with the Northern Lights Opera Company of Manitoba, this seemed like an ideal jumping off point.

Job one: Get settled, get started, get going. *(I know. I know. That's three jobs.)* Off to the Ratison Hotel, followed by a check-in with the Winnipeg Opera in The Century Concert Hall, calling on the orchestra director and his staff, and nailing down rehearsal times and space. All this has been going smoothly except for the interference of Honoria Heifer. There are divas and egos galore in the world of music but this cow has advanced degrees in self-admiration and pushy meddling. She is with us at the behest of the Bearoness, but I'm certain Belinda had no idea of the nightmare she had unleashed. Unfortunately, she's down for the gestation count (8 months) and can't be reached to turn off this bovine blitzkrieg. We shall have to devise other strategies.

Maury Meerkat

Chapter One

Monday Evening – Winnipeg, Manitoba

Well, this case is unfolding right now.
Since that artsy, ridiculous cow
Made a terrible goof.
(Open mouth, insert hoof!)
Boy, she started a terrible row!

"And that wraps up the CWP-TV Evening News Edition for Winnipeg, Manitoba, Churchill and beyond. Join us again at eleven, won't you. This is Morley Moose wishing you the very best of Monday evenings. It's just eight o'clock so stay tuned for Beatrice Beaver as she brings us up to date on the latest and greatest in Arts, Entertainment, Life Styles and Animal Interest Stories on "Bea's Beat." *(Music Up and Out)* "Hi Bea, anything we should give a dam aboot?"

"Morley, that joke hash more hair than you do. Fire your writersh! And yesh, tonight we have sheveral shtories you're going to like. Preparashuns for the Annual Beshtiary Ball. A new film – not aboot penguins – and an unusual shelebrity interview. But first, these messhages…"

We were sprawled in the cocktail lounge of the Winnipeg Ratison Hotel winding down after a hectic day of rehearsals and preparations, paying little or no attention to the round hairy face with glistening capped teeth beaming out at us from the 3-D high definition screen when Bearyl slopped her bowl of frozen daiquiri and shouted, "Hey, isn't this the show where Honoria's being interviewed?"

We grabbed our drinks and pushed, pulled and otherwise propelled our seats closer to the TV set. We were the only patrons in the bar so we had no compunction about turning up the volume.

While a sweet little deer babbles on aboot soapy little bubbles and other cutesy ads try to part us from our farthings, let me take a moment and introduce our company here in the lounge.

Ladies first: The soon to be famous polaratura soprano, Bearnice Blanc and her twin sister, Bearyl, a budding actress. These two gorgeous examples of polar pulchritude are wonders to behold. They are also members of Belinda's all-star troupe, *The Aquabears*, a swimming, diving, acrobatic, strutting group of showbears that have been appearing worldwide in the blockbuster revue, "*Some Like It Cold.*"

With them is a Himalayan Snow Leopard named Lepi (Leperello) who is, in addition to being Bearnice's baritone singing partner, an operatic composer, rock musician *(cf. Volumes Two and Three – The Case of the Spotted Band and The Case of Scotch)* and a beautiful hunk who usually has the female members of the audience slobbering in their seats. Lepi escaped from China when things got too hot for him after he unleashed his opera, *Comrade Carmen's Carbuncle*, which dealt not too kindly with the regime. We first met him in Brazil during Carnaval.

The aforementioned Madame Honoria Heifer from the Edinbeargh Opera is their bearly welcome voice coach and all around pain in the ass. She is working *(?)* with the two budding stars and accompanying our tour at Bearoness Belinda's behest. She had somehow wheedled herself an interview on *"Bea's Beat"* on Monday night in anticipation of Bearnice and Lepi's recitals over the coming weekend.

Oops! The commercials are ending. Bea is back.

"And now here's Rochelle Raccoon with the latest on the upcoming Beshtiary Ball!"

OK, I think we can do without Rochelle. But while we're on the subject of the Bestiary Ball, some years ago Belinda Black got her start in show biz by knocking everyone dead at the Ball when she made her debut in a crocodile costume. Her stage-struck mother pushed her into the *Aquabear Revue* and then into the paws of the fabulously wealthy Polar Bearon Byron Bruin, much to the distress of Octavius. The Great Bear had met and romanced Belinda earlier while doing research on polar bears in Churchill. Momma Black put the kibosh on that union. Then, when she learned that the playboy Bearon not only owned the *Aquabear Revue* but half of the remaining universe, she pushed the new aqueuse, Belinda Béarnaise, down the aisle and up the social register.

The marriage didn't last long. The Bearon was killed in an avalanche while skiing down a slope filming a Pola-Cola commercial. The widow, now Bearoness Belinda Béarnaise Bruin *(nee Black)*, after an appropriate period of mourning, literally got her act together and returned to the Aquabears as owner and star performer. It was at a charity show that she met Octavius again. After a stop-start, paw's length relationship and a few wild adventures, they finally eloped and got married back here in Canada. Belinda isn't with us in Winnipeg. She's back at Bearmoral Castle, her bearonial manse and soon-to-be luxury Shetland Islands hotel, in pre-natal hibernation.

At last, Rochelle has finished gushing all over herself and several young, fetching fauna females who it seems, will make their debut at the gala. Bea is back.

"And now, as I'm shure you all know thish Shaturday night will mark the return to the Manitoba mushical shtage of one of our own...the lovely polaratura sow, Bearnishe Blanc, who after shinging sheveral years with the Northern Lights Opera Company, joined the *Aquabear Revue* along with her beautiful twin shister, Bearyl, an aspiring actress. Did you know these ladies also pilot the last remaining Concorde EshEshTee owned by another of Winnipeg's favorite daughters, the immenshely beautiful, talented and veeeery rich, Bearonessh Belinda Béarnaishe Bruin *(nee Black?)* At this moment. the Bearonessh is tucked away in her shtately Shetland eshtate where rumor hath it that she is expecting cubs. She was shecretly married in Churchill last year to the fabuloush gazzilionaire, Octavius Bear. So now, Belinda, as all her friendsh call her, has added another name to her lengthy collection of B's – Bear."

"Immediately before the concert we'll be interviewing Bearnishe and her hunky baritone shinging partner, Lepi, a Himalayan Shnow Leopard (Wait till you shee him, girls!) But tonight, we're fortunate to have with ush, their vocal coach, Madame Honoria Heifer of the Edinbeargh Opera. Madame Heifer, welcome."

"Ummmooo! It is my pleasure, indeed, Ms Beaver. Those of us who worship at the altars of the muses Erato, Aoide and Euterpe are always delighted to have the opportunity to share our considered thoughts with others, whether they are operatically inclined or not. I am extraordinarily delighted to introduce my two operatic protégés to you here in Canada, Ms Bearnice Blanc and Mr. Leperello who are making their very first professional debuts outside of Scotland."

"Well, Madame Heifer, that's not exactly true. Bearnishe sang for sheveral years with our own Northern Lights Opera Company and I undershtand that Mr. Leperello was a sholoist with the People's Opera in China and is a composher as well."

"Umoooo! I did say 'professional,' Ms Beaver. You simply cannot compare the two raw talents who were originally placed in my expert hooves to the much more polished performers who will grace your stage this weekend. They were indeed, like some many amatoors, eager and endowed with unformed potential. But it is only an exceptional, perceptive and persuasive artiste like myself who could refine their modest capabilities. I sh-udder to think of them still wasting away as just another pair of musical mediocrities. Oh no, professionalism must be inspired and taught, Ms Beaver. And while my struggling protégés are only at the early stages of their journey, I feel great pride in being able to guide their faltering paws toward, we hope, eventual stardom."

I'm not sure what the toothy interviewer said in response because Bearyl jumped up and yanked the TV cable out of the wall. Lepi and Bearnice were both on their feet in a rage, roaring and growling in unison and I, their faithful agent, was trying to calm them down. (Rule One: Always protect the talent from seriously damaging themselves.)

However, the odds on a two foot tall meerkat restraining a livid leopard and a wildly p-o'd polar bear without doing serious damage to *himself* are quite slim. Therefore, I was not surprised to find myself rolling snout over paws across the floor. Bruised and bloody, sure, but not surprised.

"Musical mediocrities!! Faltering paws!! What colossal nerve! I'll kill her. That... that cow!! So help me, I'll rip her apart. Just let me get my claws into that mega-rumped bitch and there'll be free steaks for the entire population of Winnipeg." This was Bearnice.

Lepi was snarling dramatically in Chinese which, thank the gods, no one else understood. Bearyl, after taking another good-luck swipe at the TV, turned and, seeing me on the floor tangled up in the bar rail, stomped over. Hauling me none too gently to my feet, she grabbed a stack of cocktail napkins from the panic-stricken bartender and planted them on my bleeding ear. The two of us turned just in time to catch Bearnice and Lepi bounding out of the lounge, through the crowded lobby and into the street (knocking over a walrus and a couple of Siberian Husky bell-hops on the way.)

"Bearnice, Lepi! Come back!" Bearyl shouted (and I squeaked) as we ran after them. That is, she ran. My tail got stuck in the revolving door. After finally yanking it loose, I spun street-ward and barreled into Bearyl. She was squinting up and down the sidewalks and into the busy traffic. Neither one of them in sight! I turned to question the Door Dog but his attention was taken up with helping an inebriated buffalo out of a taxi. Clean getaway!!

Bearyl looked at me. "My sister has a temper."

I would never have known.

Octavius

The Development of Civilization-Volume 4 Part 2
Quantum Leaps?

(From "An Introduction to Faunapology" by Octavius Bear Ph.D.)

I regard myself as one of the few members of the scientific community to have a comprehensive grasp of quantum mechanics, the scientific principles addressing the infinitesimal. I also am deeply steeped in Newtonian physics Phigg Newton - (1643-1727) as well as Albeart Einstein's (1875-1955) remarkable work expanding Newton's pronouncements dealing with the nature of the infinite but tangible universe. However, somewhere between the very, very small and the unimaginably large, there is a major disconnect among the theorists. Quantum mechanics and Newtonian physics don't match up! There have been attempts to patch over the gaps with approaches like string, thread, rope, cable, twine, wire, filament, chain and cord theories. In the process, the theoretical multiverse has acquired as many as eleven dimensions including space - time.

There is one principle of quantum theory that should interest us at this point in our narrative. Quantum superposition at the sub-atomic level.

In 1935, a cat named Schrodinger showed how superposition would operate in the every day world. As long as we do not observe or measure it, an object can exist in any number (a superposition) of states. It is only when we turn our attention to the object that the superposition is lost, and the object appears in only one of its potential states. This situation is sometimes called quantum indeterminacy or the observer's paradox: the observation or measurement itself affects an outcome, so that the outcome as such does not exist unless the measurement is made.

Can this explain the possibility of us visiting parallel universes? If a witness, after shutting down all sensory perception through sleep or coma, totally withdraws from observing the current world, can this same sense-deprived observer then somehow "change channels" and have a different universe appear to his reawakened senses? Is this how hibernating bears and deep sleep subjects like Wyatt Where make quantum leaps from one parallel world to another? Can we all do it? Do we want to? Can I do it during my narcoleptic outages? Do I want to? Damned if I know!

Chapter Two

Tuesday Morning– The Bear's Lair: Cincinnati

Here's our crime-fighting Hero, the Bear,
Taking charge in his opulent Lair.
He will soon sally forth
Heading up to the North
And another brain-teasing affair.

Frau Ilse Schuylkill, a to-die-for lupine beauty, who is also Octavius Bear's housekeeper, cordon bleu chef, security officer, part-time detective, chief pilot and manager of the Bear's Lair's many facilities, padded into the Great Bear's office, growled gently and said, "Your pardon, Herr Bear. I have the latest reports from Bearmoral Castle for you."

"Thank you, Frau. *(Octavius could never bring himself to call her Ilse. Indeed, with a few exceptions, none of us could. It was only recently we had found out her first name after Colonel Wyatt Where, another wolf and the Frau's romantic interest had casually dropped it in a conversation.)*

"The Bearoness is sleeping well and comfortably. She is being attended to by her castle staff. The castle renovations are going smoothly and on time. *(Bearmoral Castle started life as a theme park. Belinda's status-conscious grandfather in-law then converted it into an "ancestral" castle for the Bruin family whose purchased "nobility" stretched back all of three generations. After throwing out her phony in-laws in Volume Three – The*

25

Case of Scotch, she proceeded to reestablish the castle as a luxury hotel and theme park. Work goes on during her hibernation.)

"Any news from the Winnipeg contingent?"

"Everyone arrived safely and well. Herr Maury says all the arrangements are working out. The one problem is that verdammte cow, Honoria Heifer. She is annoying everyone and doing nothing worthwhile."

"I'm not sure what Bel had in mind when she hired that damned bovine to coach the kids. I think I'll have a few words with that lowing menace when we go north later this week. I'll remind her where her fees are coming from. How are our travel arrangements working out?"

"All will be in readiness, Herr Bear. The Ursa Major is *startbereit,* sorry, good-to-go! Have you decided who should go with you?"

"Well, certainly you and Colonel Where. You'll be piloting the plane. I know Otto wants to come and so does L. Condor. Bruce is back in Australia. That leaves Howard and of course Marlin, our dolphin friend. Bringing him along in his tank is too much logistics for such a short trip. But I'd like to have someone on the staff here in case of an emergency. I think I'll ask Howard to stay behind. Is he around? I could use an update on the Multiverse Project."

"I'll call him, Herr Bear." She disappeared for a moment and then flashed back into the room. "He's on his way." *(Hyperspeed on display.)*

By the way, have we had any news about Chita?" *(Narrator's Note: You will meet all of these worthies shortly.)*

"I think she's up to her spotted behind in getting her oil rig going and getting the first issues of her magazines published. Since Dame Bearbi was arrested for trying to murder the Bearoness, our Chita seems to have taken over Da Savile Row enterprises. I keep waiting for the British Police to arrest her for all of her own crimes."

"That cat not only has nine lives or more. She seems able to be totally elusive in broad daylight and right in front of the constabulary. She'll be in big trouble, though, if she shows her feline face back here in the States."

"I wouldn't put anything past her," growled the Frau. "I'm sorry I didn't get a chance to go one-on-one with her in Las Vegas or back here. Don't be surprised if she shows up in Canada."

"Nothing that cat does will surprise me."

Howard walked into the room, waved at the Frau and settled down on one of the special benches designed to accommodate his spines. *(Howard is a porcupine. A super-genius porcupine but still stuck with his quills. I know, I know, terrible pun.)*

"Howard, I'm heading up to Winnipeg to support Lepi and Bearnice's recital. The Frau, Colonel, Otto and L. Condor will be joining me. I need someone back here to take charge. I'd like that to be you. We should be back by next Monday. I'm sure Marlin will supply you with company and a lot of intellectual support but he's rather limited in his ability to get around *(small chuckle.)* Do you have any problems with staying behind? I know we've emptied the Lair before for serious missions but I'm still not comfortable that our friend Imperius, the loony duck is indeed out of the picture. In fact, lacking any real evidence of his death, I prefer to act as if he's still out there somewhere plotting his next crazy scheme. Although he's less of a threat by himself, that baboon can also spell trouble."

"No problem at all, Octavius. If Imperius or Bigg show their faces, we'll be ready for them and I'd welcome the opportunity to devote some more extended research time to the Multiverse Project."

(Readers of Volumes One, Two and Three of this series may remember that Octavius has become increasingly convinced that other universes exist beyond our own. He is further convinced that some levels of inter-world contact have already been established, in many cases, accidentally. Three members of our own team, Colonel Wyatt Where; Juno, Octavius' mother; and Agrippa, his half brother all have had experiences strongly indicating other worlds exist. Two of those cases have also led us to assume that Homo Sapiens, who perished long ago on our Earth, may be alive, and possibly even dominant, in some parallel universes. To further investigate these suppositions, Octavius has organized Project Multiverse and put our porcupine scientific whiz kid, Howard Watt in charge of the research effort. Of course, Octavius being Octavius, he was not about to sit back and simply watch as Howard did his work. Howard's major thrust thus far has been gathering, analyzing and synthesizing what has turned out to be a much more substantial body of global evidence than anyone had supposed. He was now entering an extrapolation phase. Stay tuned.)

"Good," said the Great Bear. "We'll keep in touch while I'm away."

"Why am I not surprised?" thought the porcupine.

The private line on the bear's speaker phone rang. The caller ID was from my cell. Octavius pressed the talk button and roared, "Bear here." *(Octavius believed he had to bellow on the top of his formidable lungs when using a speaker phone. All attempts to convince him otherwise went nowhere.)*

"Octavius? Maury! We have a serious problem here!"

Chapter Three

Tuesday Morning – Winnipeg

Yes, the Heifer is certainly dead
From a terrible blow to her head.
Let us bid her good-bye
But "who-dunnit" and why?
Do you think it was something she said?

"Here is a breaking news item exclusive to CWP-TV News for Winnipeg, Manitoba, Churchill and beyond. This morning, the battered, dead carcass of a well dressed cow was found in an alleyway near the studios of CWP-TV. Local police have tentatively identified the victim as Madame Honoria Heifer, well-known voice coach from Edinbeargh, Scotland. She arrived in Winnipeg yesterday with polaratura soprano Bearnice Blanc and her baritone partner Mr. Leperello, a Himalayan Snow Leopard. They are scheduled to give performances this Saturday evening and Sunday afternoon with the Winnipeg Opera at the Century Hall.

Madame Heifer was last seen alive last night here at the CWP-TV studios after she concluded an interview with our own Beatrice Beaver. She was staying at the Ratison Hotel.

Because of the international aspects of this case as well as the fame of the victim, the Royal Canadian Unmounted Police have been called in to lead the investigation. We expect to hear from RCUP Superintendent Rowan

Caballus at a news conference currently scheduled for noon, Central Standard Time. Stay with us here at CWP-TV as this story unfolds…"

Leaving the TV on, I skittered down the hall to the suite shared by Bearyl and Bearnice, pausing at Lepi's door to get him out of bed. I rapped on the bears' door and waited. Bearnice or Bearyl *(they're identical twins)* opened the door a crack, saw it was me and stepped aside to let me run in. The two polars were up and around and just getting ready to go down for breakfast.

Catching my breath, I blurted, "Honoria's dead! I heard it on TV."

Lepi chose that moment to come bounding through the still open door, looked at me and said, "Repeat that. Honoria's dead?"

Choruses of "How, when, where?" *(no why?)*

I replied in order "Don't know, don't know, near the TV station. They suspect foul play. Her body was badly battered. The police and the RCUP are on it. News Conference at noon."

All three blew out their breath at the same moment, the equivalent of a Beaufort 8 gale.

"Well, I can't say I'm sorry she's gone." This from Bearnice. "She was driving the two of us into a rage. Oh, sorry. Bad choice of words. But I just wanted her to get on the next jet and flown back to Edinbeargh. I wish I could have reached Belinda but she's out for the count. But I didn't want the cow dead…in spite of what I may have said last night in the bar."

31

She and Lepi stared at each other and then at Bearyl and me. "Ohmigod, that bartender and half the lobby heard us ranting about her. I even threatened to make steaks out of her."

Lepi scratched his head, sighed and said, "Well I guess that's going to put the two of us pretty high up on the suspect list."

In one of those ridiculous coincidences that only happen in murder mysteries, there came a rap on the half open door. Two local constables and an officer of the RCUP, brandishing weapons, stormed into the room. The Unmountie bellowed. "Ms Bearnice Blanc, Mr. Leperello. You are under arrest on suspicion of the murder of Madame Honoria Heifer. I must warn you that anything you say may be used against you."

I took my life in my hands and walked up to the horse and said, "I'm Mauritius Meerkat, agent for Ms Blanc and Mr. Leperello. They will say nothing until they are properly represented by legal council. In the meantime, let me advise you that you have arrested the wrong bear."

"That's what they all say!"

"No, seriously, your pawcuffs are on Ms Bearnice Blanc's twin sister, Bearyl. Unless you have a warrant for *her* arrest, may I suggest you release her immediately."

"So, how the hell do we tell them apart?"

"Bearnice wears an ankle bracelet and she sings."

Chapter Four

Tuesday Morning - Still Winnipeg

This bad news has me really distressed
Our young singers are under arrest.
Since a bartender's claim
Says that they are to blame.
But the two of them haven't confessed.

Bearyl went with Bearnice and Lepi to the police station. I stayed behind and immediately got on the horn to The Great Bear.

"Octavius? Maury! We have serious problem here! It looks like Honoria Heifer has been murdered and the police have jumped the gun on the say-so of a hotel bartender and have arrested Bearnice and Lepi on suspicion of..."

The Bear snorted *(loudly)* and roared into the speaker phone. "OK. Let's take this from the top."

I played back last night's episode in the hotel bar, starting with Honoria's TV interview and ending up standing in the street with Bearyl trying to see where Bearnice and Lepi had run off to. I told Octavius that including the bartender, there were a number of witnesses to the polar and pardine *(Lepi is not a feline.)* fury and their violent exit from the hotel apparently in search of Honoria.

After some more futile searching, Bearyl and I had returned to the hotel and went to our respective rooms. Neither Lepi nor Bearnice were back. I was sure their anger would blow over. After all, this was just the latest in the heifer's constant stream of irritating posturings. *(I was surprised one of them didn't try to push her out of the SST on the way over. Just kidding!)* I guessed they had stopped somewhere and blew off steam with a couple of drinks.

Then I turned on the TV this morning and heard the announcement. I ran into the polars' room with the news and Lepi joined us. That's when the arrest took place. I don't know what's happening at the Police station. Bearyl is there and she said she'd try to get a lawyer.

It wasn't time yet for the promised press conference.

Octavius interrupted my sorry tail at that point and asked who was in charge of the investigation. I told him it was Superintendent Rowan Caballus of the RCUP.

"I've worked with him." said the Bear. "He's a bit of a stiff but he's a good cop. Not likely to go off the deep end without making his case airtight. All right! Looks like I'm going to Winnipeg earlier than I thought. I'll check in with the Frau and The Colonel and let you know how soon I can get up there. The Ursa Major is all ready for the trip so it shouldn't be very long. Probably late this afternoon. I'll call you back when we're on our way. Get us some rooms and see how much more you can find out about what Bearnice and Lepi really did last night, if you can get to talk to them. Which TV station will air the press conference? I'll see if L. Condor can hook into it."

I told him and we both hung up.

*****

"This is CWP-TV News - Morley Moose reporting. We are live at Winnipeg Police Headquarters, awaiting the arrival of Superintendent Rowan Caballus of the RCUP who will make a statement aboot the sudden and brutal death of the famous international music authority, Madame Honoria Heifer. All of Winnipeg, indeed all of Manitoba, was shocked at what seems to be a bovinicide in our usually quiet and low crime city. Theories abound on what happened and who was involved. Hopefully, the police will be forthcoming aboot the event, the perpetrator or perpetrators and the motivation behind this heinous crime. Oh, the Superintendent is now approaching the podium."

A tall, robust black and white horse, *(a blue roan)* wearing the distinctive Red Serge uniform of the RCUP, amply decorated with campaign ribbons, badges and the stripes and stars of a high ranking Superintendent of Police, took his place behind the microphones, shook his head, whinnied and in a clear, rumbling voice said, "Good day, gentlebeasts of the press. I am Superintendent Rowan Caballus of the RCUP. I have been assigned the task of managing our investigation into the untimely death of Madame Honoria Heifer of Edinbeargh, Scotland. Madame Heifer was here in Winnipeg to direct the singing recital this weekend of Ms Bearnice Blanc, a Polar Bear soprano and Mr. Leperello, a Himalayan Snow Leopard baritone. Ms Blanc is a former member of our Northern Lights Opera but more recently has been in the employ of the world-famous Bearoness Belinda Béarnaise Bruin Bear (nee Black) of Bearmoral Castle in the Shetland Islands. Mr. Leperello is a political émigré from China also living with the Bearoness. We currently have both of these individuals in custody pending further investigation of the events."

(Mutterings, paws and hooves raised, shouted questions from the audience.)

"I am sorry but I cannot supply any further information aboot these individuals at this time or why we are holding them other than to say testimony from several witnesses have led us to believe that they may have some involvement in this murder. As to the death of Madame Heifer, our crime scene unit and representatives from the coroner's office have determined that in view of the nature of her wounds and overall condition of her body at the time of her demise, neither natural causes or accident seem to be likely. Indeed, the evidence points to a vicious clawed attack ending in her skull being fractured by a heavy, blunt instrument. We do not have the weapon at this moment. She was found in an alley adjacent to the studios of CWP-TV where she had granted an interview earlier in the evening. The coroner's staff tentatively estimates the time of death to be somewhere around ten PM. Unfortunately, the security camera system at CWP has been down for the last several days for upgrading and so we have no evidence from that source. We have prepared briefing papers for each of you. I will not take questions at this time. Thank you very much." *(Grumbling, pushing and shoving to get the briefing papers, shouted questions, general noise and stirring.)*

"This is Morley Moose back again. Well, Superintendent Caballus was not as forthcoming or enlightening as we might have hoped. We are especially intrigued by the police holding Ms Blanc and Mr. Leperello on suspicion. And who are these witnesses whose testimony has caused them to be held? As events progress, count on CWP-TV News to keep you informed. And now back to our regularly scheduled programming."

*****

Maury here! Time to do a little investigating on my own while I wait for Octavius and the team to arrive. First thing: Find Bearyl. Last I knew she had gone to the Police Station with Bearnice and Lepi. I called her cell phone and she told me she was just leaving on her way back to the hotel. The RCUP hadn't interrogated either of them yet. They were waiting for the court to appoint an attorney. She did get a chance to talk to the two of them privately and got the story on where they went and what they did after bolting out of the hotel. We decided to hold off that conversation until we were face to face. Never know who might be intercepting our phones. I told her Octavius was on his way. I need to get some rooms and ground facilities laid on.

Chapter Five

Mid-day Tuesday - Aboard the Ursa Major

The Bear's lawyer went fast as could be
To confer with the RCUP.
With the singers in tow,
You'll be happy to know
That he managed to get them set free

The C-5A had just completed its rollout and taken up a north-northwest heading for Winnipeg. Estimated flying time: two and a half hours. On board were Frau Schuylkill and Colonel Where in the cockpit and Octavius in his modified cargo pod. Otto and L. Condor rounded out the passenger list. Also in the hold of the aircraft were two utility vehicles and a truck for transporting Octavius. Howard the Porcupine Genius had stayed behind to hold down the fort with Marlin, the Dolphin on sabbatical leave from the court of the Prince of Whales to work with us on undersea communications.

L. Condor had captured a replay of the televised statement by the RCUP Superintendent. The Great Bear was heating up the atmosphere with calls to the Canadian border authorities to get clearances for the party and the vehicles. He was also contacting several Manitoba law firms he knew to get the two singers the best criminal representation available. Cost no object. He placed a courtesy call to Superintendent Caballus to let him know he wished to join in the investigation. The reception was polite but unenthusiastic. The Super knew Octavius well enough from prior cases to realize he would not be able to wave the Bear off if he was determined to stick his big black nose in the enquiry. Finally, he called me, told me who was coming with him and instructed Bearyl and me to stand by for a war council as soon as they arrived at the Ratison.

As they approached Winnipeg Airport, he got confirmation that the law firm of Fox, Fox and Fox had sprung into action. They were currently engaged in getting Bearnice and Lepi released on the basis that no actual evidence connected them to the murder – just hearsay from several hotel employees. However, they were asked to surrender their passports even though their up-coming concert made it very unlikely they would be flight-risks, to say nothing of Octavius' reputation as their sponsor.

*****

After a typical Canadian customs and border hassle, they came rolling up to the entrance to the Ratison Hotel, just as Lepi and Bearnice were getting out of a limo with a well dressed fox in the lead. Octavius tumbled out of the truck bed and shambled over to the trio. He shook paws with Lepi, gave Bearnice a gentle *(for him)* hug and turned to the fox. Standing erect at his full nine foot *(2.7432 meters)* height, he rumbled, "Good afternoon, I am Octavius Bear. I guess I am your client although these young folks are the ones who need your legal help. I have told Superintendent Caballus to expect investigative help from my colleagues and me."

"Good evening, Doctor Bear. *(Good start! always hit him with Ph.D.'s)* I am Forrest F. Fox, partner and lead criminal counsel at the firm of Fox, Fox, and Fox. I will be personally handling this case. May I suggest we go inside, allow you to get settled and then strategize our next moves. I believe your assistant has made arrangements here at the hotel."

Cue the Meerkat! I had been standing in the Ratison lobby with Bearyl awaiting the ursine invasion. Surrounded by several bell dogs and the desk manager, we hustled the team and their baggage into the hotel, heading for the elevators. The valet parking cats took our three vehicles. A small crowd had gathered both outside and inside the lobby, staring at our entourage. The real object of the gawking and gaping was, as usual, the huge Kodiak who seemed to be in charge.

Twenty minutes later after dumping *(literally)* their baggage in their rooms and "freshening up," the team descended on a conference room located away from the lobby traffic. Forrest Fox seemed somewhat overwhelmed; first, by the number of participants and second, by the wide range of species. L. Condor came in for some special staring. Octavius, as usual, led off the discussion. "First, I'll do a round of introductions. I think, Mr. Fox, that first name basis would facilitate things, if you have no objection. I'm Octavius."

"Certainly, Doctor Bear, er, Octavius. Please call me Forrest."

"Fine. You've already met our two singers, Bearnice and Leperello, who incidentally prefers 'Lepi.' I'm not sure whether you have met Bearyl Blanc, Bearnice's twin sister. Bearyl is an actress. Both ladies are members of the world famous Aquabear Troupe that is owned and directed by my recent bride, Bearoness Belinda Béarnaise Bruin Bear (nee Black) of Bearmoral Castle in the Shetlands. Unfortunately for this case, Belinda is undergoing pre-natal hibernation. She would have been a major asset in this situation. These two ladies also pilot the aircraft belonging to the Bearoness, especially her Concorde SST. We may wish to soft pedal that to keep the flight-risk issue from rearing its ugly head.

This gentlebeast is Mauritius Meerkat, 'Maury.' He is my right paw animal both in helping me run my extensive enterprises as well assisting in my investigations. He is also the theatrical agent for Bearnice and Lepi. These two wolves are, respectively, Frau Ilse Schuylkill and Colonel Wyatt Where, Retired. *(Wonder of wonders. For the very first time in my hearing, he used the Frau's first name.)* Among their many talents, the ones pertinent to this event are their experience in security, investigation and if necessary, use of weapons. They also pilot my aircraft.

This otter, whose theatrical name is Otto the Magnificent, has a number of very unique talents we may feel called upon to utilize. I'll say no more about that for the moment. Finally, our recent friend from Brazil, L. Condor is one of the world's leading computing and telecommunications experts. It was he who downloaded copies of Madame Honoria's interview and the RCUP press conference for our review on the way up here."

Paw and wing shakes all around.

"Now," he rumbled, "What the hell is going on here??"

Cacophony as Bearnice, Lepi, Bearyl, Forrest and I all tried to take the floor. Octavius put up his massive paws to stop the noise and looked to Forrest. "Before we launch into a narrative of events, can you explain the legal situation for us?"

"At the moment, Bearnice and Lepi are released in their own recognizance on condition they do not leave Winnipeg. Thus far, nothing found at the crime scene directly connects them to the cow's death. Her wounds could have been caused by any number of sharp claws or devices. A blunt instrument, as yet unfound, was used to finish her off. There were no incriminating traces of blood or other materials on either Bearnice or Lepi. Now, the police are quick to insist that since they had ample time before being arrested to bathe, destroy their clothing and remove any other signs of violence, the lack of such evidence proves nothing. Fortunately, the burden of proof is on the authorities."

"I plan to meet with Superintendent Caballus as soon as possible," said the Bear. "I have urged him to allow me to directly join in the investigation. He is of two minds on the subject, but in the past he has found me both helpful and difficult to dissuade."

"At the moment," said the Fox, "the principle evidence, if you want to call it that, comes from the hotel bartender who swears both of them went into a rage on hearing the Heifer's interview and threatened to turn her into steaks. He said that they rushed from the bar and left the hotel in a great hurry. That part is borne out by several other hotel employees. No witnesses to the actual event near the television studios so far. At best circumstantial and hearsay but who knows what the police will discover next."

Octavius again. "Bearyl and Maury! You were there, right? Forget about your own feelings for them. Does your experience match the bartender's statement?"

Hesitant "yeses" from both of us. "But that doesn't mean anything except they were angry."

"And ran out of the hotel." the Bear rejoined. "Look, you two. You may well be called on to back up the bartender's story. That's uncomfortable but you'll have to tell at least a minimum version of the truth."

At this point, Lepi snarled. "Just a damned minute! When do we get to tell our version of this mess? Bearnice and I were nowhere near the TV studios or Honoria. There was nothing for us to clean up because we didn't do anything. The police claim she was killed around ten. At ten, we were in another bar not far from here, trying to calm down and figure out how to ditch her from our program. We decided we were going to lay that one on you, Maury. You _are_ our agent."

Bearnice chimed in. "OK, the bartender's story as far as it goes is basically true. We had had it up to here with that overweening cow. Between her endless bitching, her constant ego trips and her laying it on with Opera management, she was turning from being a distraction to being a real menace."

Forrest sucked in his breath. "I think, Bearnice, that you will want to get those words out of your vocabulary. You're just amplifying the motive angle and we already have too much of that to contend with. Where was this bar you were decompressing in and would anyone remember you?"

"It's just five or six blocks from here. I don't remember the name. Do you, Lepi?

Negative head shake.

"We can certainly find it again."

"How long were you there?"

"I don't know. The interview was on at about 8:20 or so and I guess we rushed out of the hotel at about 8:30. After a couple of minutes, we realized we didn't know where the TV studio was or even if Honoria would still be there. When we had caught our breaths, we decided we'd take it up in the morning. We found ourselves outside this bar and thought we could use a drink or two while we figured out exactly how to get rid of her. *(Choking sounds from Forrest and Octavius.)* Oh, Sorry! Wrong words! The big problem was the Bearoness. She had engaged Honoria and was paying for her services, such as they were. I'm sure she would have sided with us but we couldn't check with her and this bitch cow wasn't going to leave without making a lot of noise. That's when we decided to dump it on Maury."

(Maury: Needless to say, I would have been absolutely enthralled by the prospect. Well, being an agent is not all beer and skittles. I'm not crazy about beer and I don't even know what skittles are.)

Forrest again: "The Police Crime Scene Unit thinks she was murdered around ten. The Medical Examiner hasn't confirmed that but do you think you were still in that bar at ten?"

"Possibly!" said Lepi, "By then we weren't feeling much pain from the drinks and we were both exhausted. We had been working with the opera staff, rehearsing and listening to Honoria for most of the day after the flight over from Scotland. Even on an SST, you can get jet lag. We sort of staggered our way back to the hotel and went to our rooms. That may have been around ten thirty or so. I'm not sure."

"Bearyl," asked Octavius, "you and Bearnice are rooming together. Do you remember her coming in?"

"No, I went to bed early. I was dead to the world. Oh, God, I said it, too."

"OK" said the Bear, "let's organize. Forrest and I will get together with the police. Maybe still this evening if we can swing it. Lepi and Bearnice! You continue on with your rehearsals and planning. Bearyl and Maury! Go with them to the center first thing in the morning. Use the 'So sad aboot Honoria but the show must go on.' routine. If you get any pushback, I'm sure you can handle it."

(His confidence level was a hell of lot higher than mine.)

"Senhor Condor! Can you and Otto poke around the TV station and see what you can find out about the interview before, during and after? Otto, you might want to use your talent for getting in and out of places to look into the physical set-up including the alley, which I'm sure has been cordoned off as a crime scene."

Otto winked.

"Frau and Colonel! See what, if anything further you can find out from the hotel staff. As soon as I can make nice-nice with the Superintendent, we can go into active mode. Then we'll all be very busy. There's a nasty killer or killers involved here and we don't know what to expect. We have to wrap this up in a few days in order to make sure the Saturday and Sunday recitals go on as scheduled."

Chapter Six

Tuesday Evening - RCUP Headquarters

The Great Bear wants to get in the act
To find out how the cow was attacked.
Let his crime fighting team
Solve the murderous scheme.
How will Rowan Caballus react?

"Good evening Rowan. Thanks for making time for us. You know Mr. Fox?"

"Of course! Hello Forrest! And hello again to you, Octavius. Welcome to Winnipeg. No point in my asking why you're here. You seem to be convinced that your two protégés had nothing to do with the cow's murder in spite of the testimony of the hotel staff."

Forrest broke in, "All that testimony suggests is that they were upset at Madame Heifer's self aggrandizing comments. A rather natural reaction, I should say."

"And I should say that they were more than upset. 'Enraged' was the word the bartender used. Pulling the cable from the TV, overturning chairs, pitching your Mr. Meerkat onto the floor and causing him to bleed, racing through the lobby and crashing into several of the staff in their haste. There's heap of motive right there."

"All circumstantial, Rowan," said the Great Bear. "I'll grant you they were angry but unless you have made some breakthroughs in the last few hours, there is nothing to tie them to the murder scene, much less the event. They told us they didn't even know where the TV station was and after running a few blocks, they collapsed. They'd been up most of the night before, flying from the Shetlands. They spent most of the day, working through their program with the Opera Director and his staff while listening to Honoria's nonsense. They did not have dinner and that last blast on TV was the straw that broke the Dromedary's back. After settling down, they went into a bar near the hotel to decompress and see how best they could get Honoria sent back to Edinbeargh on the next jet."

"They'll have to formally testify to all of that tomorrow morning, in your presence of course, Forrest. We also have to confirm a time line on their activities against what the Medical Examiner believes was the time of death."

Forrest asked, "The last we heard, his estimate was aboot ten o'clock. Does that still hold?"

"So far," said the horse. "Based on the condition of the body."

"How was she found?" asked Octavius.

"Trash collectors came upon her at aboot six this the morning. They called the local police. They swear they didn't touch anything or take anything away. That alley smells pretty ripe at the moment. Of course, we have it cordoned off."

Thoughts of Otto the Magnificent and his teleporting abilities flashed through Octavius' brain. Depending on how much access the police were willing to give him, he might have to resort to having Otto do some independent searching. Before he joined Octavius, the otter had been undergoing experimental treatment by the evil genius Imperius Drake. With a promise of a spectacular show business career, he was actually altering Otto's DNA, physique and brain to turn him into a highly dangerous über animal, submissive only to the Mad Duck. It didn't quite work out that way and Otto escaped the Drake's talons *(yes, talons)* but retained a number of the alterations Imperius and his deadly serum had wreaked on him. One was high speed teleportation, or so it seems. Otto is still under study by the medical staff at Universal Ursine Industries. Back to the conversation.

"You haven't found any weapon or further signs of a struggle?"

"Not yet."

"Could it be she was killed elsewhere and then dumped in the alley?"

"It's a possibility we're looking into but it doesn't seem likely. It would take several large animals to move her body or someone with a fork lift. She was a hefty heifer."

"Do you know who else Honoria may have known here in Winnipeg?"

"With the exception of the Opera staff and the TV station personnel, we haven't found any other links. But it's still early. It seems that cow had a wonderful talent for irritating anyone she came in contact with."

Forrest looked over at Rowan, "As you know, Bearnice and Lepi have two recitals scheduled this weekend. That assumes that the Opera is still willing to proceed with them. I imagine they would be very reluctant to cancel. I believe both performances are almost sold out. They were a sensation in Scotland. Based on the case so far, may I have your commitment that you will not try to disrupt those events?"

The horse stared at the fox. "Commitment, No! You know I have to follow where our investigations take us. If more evidence arises that forms a stronger basis for us to believe them guilty, I'll even arrest them on stage. However, I have no intention of harassing them. But that's the only statement I'll make."

"What aboot statements to the press?"

"We've already told the press that they have been released in their own recognizance. As far as that's concerned, I'm trusting both of you to keep them in tow."

"That's a commitment I'll make," said The Bear. "I know those two and I trust them. Plus, I have a couple of members of my staff who will be acting as their bodyguards and chaperones. *(Can you say wolves?)* Overly eager members of the fourth estate will be firmly but gently discouraged in any attempt to approach them."

"I don't want to hear any complaints against you from the press."

"We've been there before. There's something about two wolves smiling that can be very dispiriting."

Octavius looked over at Forrest. "Do you have anything more you want to say or ask the Superintendent?"

"No, my concern is for my clients. I assume you are interested in trying to help solve the murder. As long as Bearnice and Lepi are not involved in anything you find, I leave that to the Superintendent and you."

The Bear turned to the RCUP Horse. "Which brings me to my final question. Since Honoria Heifer was in the employ of my wife, Bearoness Belinda Béarnaise Bruin Bear *(nee Black)* I feel an obligation to help pursue this investigation and bring her killer or killers to justice. What is your reaction to allowing my staff and me to participate in the effort?"

"My first reaction, Octavius, is to tell you and your staff to get the hell out of Manitoba as fast as that oversized airplane can take you. Assuming we find nothing further aboot them, the singers, their agent and Bearnice's twin can find their way home on their SST after we return their passports. *(He snorted.)* But knowing you and recalling our previous joint investigations, I suppose, on balance, you will be more of a help than a hindrance. Go ahead but I'll expect to be kept totally informed of your activities and results. I reserve the right to shut you down at any time and tell you to leave the country."

"Fair enough, Rowan. Can we expect to be kept in the loop by the police?"

"Yes, as long as it doesn't jeopardize our work."

"We know better than that."

The Bear stood erect as did the Horse. Needless to say, Forrest Fox looked up at them and felt a bit intimidated. Paw and hoof shakes.

Outside the station, Forrest turned to Octavius and said, "Well, that went better than I expected. I'll have to arrange for Bearnice and Lepi to come in early tomorrow and give their formal testimony. I'll let you know the arrangements and you can decide whether you want to be there."

"It will depend on what kind of progress we are making. If I do come, it will be to hear what the police have to say. I may send the wolves in my place. Frau Schuylkill and the Colonel have two of the sharpest and subtle minds I know of. If there is something going awry, they'll catch it. They can also take up their bodyguard duties while they're at it. Right now they're backtracking the statements of the hotel employees."

Chapter Seven

Tuesday Night - The Ratison Hotel

Here's the Frau and her chum, Colonel Where
Right-paw wolves of Octavius Bear,
As they try to make sense
Out of strange evidence.
They're a clever and talented pair.

Frau Ilse and Colonel Where were wrapping up talking to the hotel's night manager who had just come on shift. The Bobcat protested that he had spoken at length to the Police but the Colonel applied a little persuasive psychology. *(No threats, no arm twisting, just smiles made up of a universe of sharp teeth.)* With the exception of seeing Lepi and Bearnice running through the lobby, the rest of his comments were third hand from the evening bartender, another Bobcat. *(It may run in the family.)*

"By the way, the damage to the bar and the replacement cost of the 3D TV is going on your boss's bill. One of our bell-dogs was knocked over and picked up a few scrapes. He's not going to sue or anything but you might want to show your apologies."

Frau Schuylkill knew that the charges for the bar damage would be chump-change to the gazzilionaire Octavius, but kept that fact to herself. Talking to the bell-dog might yield a little more useful information, especially if he knew what time Lepi and Bearnice returned to the hotel. "We'd be happy to, Herr Manager. Point him out to us and we'll see what can be done."

He called over a Labrador Husky who had just finished accompanying a family of brown bears out to an airport shuttle van. The dog shook himself and trotted over to the trio. "Yes, Mr. Rufus! What can I do for you?"

"Henry, I'd like you to meet Frau Ilse Schuylkill and Colonel Wyatt Where. They are part of the group that came in with Mr. Octavius Bear earlier today. They are also connected with the twin polar bears, snow leopard and meerkat that you, shall we say, met last night as they were exiting the hotel."

"Oh right! The bear knocked me over. No real damage. A scrape or two."

"Well, Henry." drawled Wyatt, "We'd like to compensate you for any hurt and embarrassment you suffered. Was your uniform damaged at all."

"The hotel takes care of that, sir." *(The frau mentally added another couple of charges to Octavius' bill.)*

"Why don't you take a break, Henry, and you can speak with us more casually. Will that be all right, Mr. Rufus?"

"Certainly, Colonel. Things are a bit quiet right now. No running polar bears or snow leopards to deal with."

He chuckled and Wyatt resisted the urge to take a substantial bite out of his well padded backside. As the manager sauntered away, they looked around for a quiet place to talk. Henry motioned to a table off in a corner and they moved over to it.

Ilse reached into her oversized purse. *(Containing among other things, a sharpshooter's pistol which may or may not have been registered in Canada. The Frau tends to be a bit cavalier about such things.)* She pulled out a wad of money, folded it into a small packet and pushed it across the table to the Husky.

"Oh no, ma'am. That's not necessary!" he said, while eyeing the cash with eager eyes.

"Of course it is," said the Frau, "but if it makes you feel any better you can assist us in one thing. We realize you've spoken to the police…"

"Just bearly. They really didn't seem interested in me. They…"

"But we are," interrupted Wyatt. "We want to know what, if anything, happened after the bear and the snow leopard ran out of the hotel lobby. Their names are Bearnice and Lepi, by the way."

"Well, for one thing, they were immediately followed out by a meerkat and another polar bear. Are the bears twins?"

"Yes, they are. Bearnice wears an ankle bracelet to tell them apart."

"I noticed that when she knocked me over. Her hind paws just missed me. Well anyway, the other bear and the meerkat…"

"Bearyl and Maury!"

"Thank you. They just ran outside. The meerkat caught his tail in the revolving door and got stuck. I suppose when they finally reached the street they lost track of them, because a few minutes later, they came back inside, saw all the upset in the lobby and, I guess, decided to make themselves scarce. They headed for the elevators and that's the last I saw of the meerkat."

"Wait a minute," said Wyatt, "Did you see Bearyl again?"

"Yeah, after a few minutes, she came back out of the elevator, crossed the lobby and disappeared outside. I didn't think much of it at the time. I did get a look at her hind paws. No anklet. I thought maybe the other one, Bearnice, had come back while I wasn't looking but I'm pretty sure it was Bearyl. Of course, I suppose Bearnice could have taken the anklet off but I doubt it. Anyway, aboot an hour later, she came back in and went into the elevator. Then, maybe fifteen minutes after that Bearnice and the cat came in. She had the anklet on."

"Any idea what time this was?"

"Aboot ten-thirty. My shift is over at eleven and I was starting to wrap things up."

"Have you told any of this to the police?"

"Not aboot Bearyl or the return of Bearnice and what's his name? Lepi? I told you they weren't interested in me."

"Did you tell any of this to Mr. Rufus?"

"We only talked aboot the damage and my scrapes."

"Anything else you can remember, Herr Henry?"

"Not really but," pawing the wad of money, "I'll give it some more thought and get back to you. Thanks again for this."

"Thank you. You're very observant."

"I had thoughts of becoming a Police Dog or a detective but now, I'm not so sure I want to."

"Maybe we can help you with that decision. We'll talk again."

After the dog padded off, Frau Ilse looked at Wyatt and growled. "There is something very strange about Bearyl's story. She claimed she had gone to bed and was sound asleep when Bearnice returned. Maybe she was, but not for long. Do you think we should face her down with it?"

"Let's talk to Octavius first. Somebody needs to follow up on that bar the two of them claimed to be in. We need to get them an airtight alibi so the recitals can go on without any further hitches. Oh yeah! It would also be nice to find out who really killed the cow."

Chapter Eight

Early Wednesday Morning – RCUP Headquarters

Do the singers have firm alibis?
Though the bell-dog has sharp ears and eyes,
Other questions arise
From his careful replies.
Has Ms Bearyl been telling some lies?

Maury here! There was a minor mob scene around the RCUP interview rooms. Bearnice and Lepi were there with Forrest Fox. Bearyl and I had to make a brief report to the police on our actions Monday night. Octavius had decided to come along with the Frau and the Colonel as observers. That didn't sit too well with the Superintendent but wonder of wonders, Octavius just kept his mouth shut, paying more attention to what the interviewers were saying than the testimony we were giving. I don't remember the Frau or Wyatt saying a word.

Naturally, there was heavy interest first in identifying and then going to the bar Bearnice and Lepi said they had visited after they gave up looking for Honoria. If they could prove they were there on or about *(sorry, aboot)* ten o'clock, that would go a long way toward supporting their story of being nowhere near the murder. However, that little exercise would have to wait until this evening when the bar opened up. A local police sergeant was assigned the interview and the Colonel and Frau talked their way into joining him. Of course, Bearnice and Lepi would be there. Forrest Fox said he would be there as well.

Meanwhile, Bearnice, Lepi and I were due at the Opera to smooth out any ripples caused by their arrest. I think Bearyl will be tagging along. As long as the press played up the recitals and played down the mayhem, I was pretty sure we could move things along, especially without Honoria sticking her bovine nose in things. Sorry, sounds heartless but, hey, that's show biz.

Frau Ilse and Wyatt had cornered Octavius and were deep in discussion. The last I had seen of Otto and L. Condor, they were on their way to the television station to see what they could turn up. Including Forrest, we were all supposed to meet for drinks before dinner to review the events of the day and get ready to go bar *(just one)* hopping with the police.

*****

Back at the hotel, the Frau and Colonel were sitting in the Great Bear's room. Octavius was sprawled on the bed. Not lazy, just unable to stand up with the low ceilings or sit on any of the chairs. There was some doubt as to how long the bed could handle his 1400 pound weight.

"So you believe this bell-dog's story about Bearyl?"

"Why not?" said the Colonel. "He had no reason to lie or embellish the story. We had already given him some cash to cover the wear and tear on his hide and ego so he didn't have any more to gain in that department. I don't think he was trying to impress us although he did say something about becoming a cop or a detective. After his interview with the police, he said he was thinking better of it."

"I believe him," said the Frau. "My problem is what to do with his story. Should we just face Bearyl down with it and ask why she lied about *(aboot, Oh the hell with it!)* going to bed early and not hearing Bearnice come in. If she was awake, and that seems likely if they only went to the room fifteen minutes apart, she could have supported the time line Bearnice and Lepi were claiming. She's covering up something."

"Do you think she may have killed Honoria?"

"Ach! I hope not, Herr Bear. I know she hated the cow almost as much as Bearnice and Lepi but she and Maury tried to stop them from running off."

"Remember, she is an actress and a pretty good one, I'm told. She is trained in martial arts and is certainly powerful enough to kill a defenseless cow. At least, I think Honoria was defenseless. No telling really! My first impulse is to let this ride until we search out that bar tonight. Let's put Maury in the picture when he comes back from the Opera offices. He'll have been with Bearyl most of the day and may be able to shed some more light on this. Meanwhile, I think you two should take up your bodyguard duties."

Chapter Nine

Mid Wednesday Morning – The Winnipeg Opera

Though Honoria's certainly dead,
The rehearsals are going ahead.
And here's something else new.
Where there once were just two,
Now they're offering three shows instead.

Hi, Maury Meerkat here! The Manitoba Century Concert Hall offices looked like a mob scene from ***A Tail of Two Cities.*** Lepi, Bearnice, Bearyl and I had crowded into a conference room with the Opera Director, Associate Director, Communications Manager, Public Relations Manager, Security Officer, Musical Director and Orchestra Leader for the recitals. Just as we were all getting seated *(or reasonable facsimile thereof)* Frau Schuylkill and Colonel Where joined the fray, introducing themselves and explaining that they were there at the request of Octavius Bear *(nods of recognition)* and RCUP Superintendent Rowan Caballus *(more nods of recognition)* to protect the two singers while they were in Winnipeg. Since it wasn't yet known who had perpetrated the murder of Madame Heifer or why, prudence dictated that a careful watch be put on them especially since they had been under her tutelage. Stretching the truth a bit, they went on to say that the police seemed satisfied that early reports of Lepi and Bearnice being involved in the crime were patently false.

The Security Officer, Bartholomew Badger, was about to hold forth when the Opera Director, Dr. Woodrow Wolverine, interrupted. "Thank you, Colonel Where and Frau Schuylkill. While our Security Officer, Mr. Badger, can assure you our precautions here are first-class, we can ill afford an additional surveillance and protection burden. It is not uncommon for our visiting stars to have their own bodyguards so we are used to having a team like you in the Center. I trust in your professionalism not to interfere with the ongoing activities associated with these recitals. However, let us get to the most basic issue. Should the recitals go on?"

Lepi and Bearnice looked like they were going to jump out of their skins. The Frau motioned for them to cool it.

The Director continued, "There have been some concerned questions from several of our board members, especially when it seemed possible that Ms Blanc and Mr. Leperello may have, in fact, been directly involved in Madame Heifer's death. I am relieved that I can now reassure them."

No one on our team dared look at one another and I said a prayer that our premature declaration would in fact, hold true.

The wolverine went on, turning to the Associate Director, a Canada Goose. "Godfrey, I understand that both Saturday night and Sunday afternoon are nearly sold out. Is that true?"

"Yes, Doctor Wolverine. Regrettable though it is, the sensational death of Madame Heifer has actually increased the demands for tickets. We might even be able to add another performance, if that is possible."

I jumped in. "I have already met many of you. I'm Mauritius Meerkat, agent for our two highly talented young animals and also a direct associate of the world famous detective and patron of the arts, Octavius Bear. I think we will have to consider that carefully. If you have Sunday evening in mind, two performances in one day might be a significant strain on our singers' resources. Staying for another week may or may not be feasible. And of course, there is the Center's scheduling to consider."

I think Bearnice was aboot *(got it that time)* to blurt out an emphatic "Yes" when Lepi kicked her under the table. "Let's discuss this off-line,' he said.

"Now," said Dr. Wolverine, literally licking his chops over two sell-out performances, "are there any objections to proceeding with our plans as they are currently laid out? Hearing none, I suggest we conclude this meeting. Am I correct in assuming that rehearsals and other arrangements are on solid ground?"

The Musical Director and Orchestra Leader nodded agreement.

"Will the performances be televised?"

The Communications Director, a Musk Ox, said, "They will be recorded by WCP-TV for later broadcast. Date still undetermined."

"Good, good! Oh, you two wolves. Is there any further news aboot Madame Heifer's death? She was never very popular here but such a death is a terrible thing."

The Frau picked up immediately. "Had she been here before this week?'

The Goose replied. "Oh yes, she seemed to make frequent tours of international second tier opera houses, looking for young talent she could *'Develop.'* Several members of our chorus succumbed to her blandishments, usually for a very short time. A very difficult individual."

"Are any of these young talents still here?" she asked.

The Goose turned to the Musical Director and Orchestra Leader. "Perhaps you can help these two wolves with that after we break up this meeting."

On cue, the meeting broke up. Bearnice, Lepi, Bearyl and the Colonel went along with the Orchestra Leader, a Snowshoe Hare named Hartley, to one of the rehearsal rooms to do further work on the program.

The Frau and I joined the Musical Director, Herr Professor Doktor Dieter von Tripp, an Austrian Red Stag. The Frau was mightily impressed by the impresario. "Herr Professor, how long have lived in Canada?"

"All my life. I was born here."

"Forgive me, I thought a Red Stag with an Austrian name and credentials might have hailed from Vienna, Linz or Salzburg."

"Never been to any of them. The name and title are imposing though, aren't they? It helps no end among the music snobs here of whom there are multitudes. Now let's see if I can dig up a few names of Madame Heifer's former clients for you. We like to keep track of the training and performance history of all of our singers and players. Looks great in the Playbills."

He powered up a desktop computer with a specially designed mouse and oversized keyboard, and did a lookup on Honoria Heifer. "Hmm, here's something interesting. It looks like several of our singers studied with her for short periods but there is nothing in here on Madame Heifer, herself. If she had a singing career, there's no mention of it. Not all vocal coaches start out as performers, of course, but if memory serves, she was never shy aboot *(aha!)* making great claims for her musical prowess."

"Let's see, five names over the last seven years. None of them are on staff with us now. In fact, if they are still singing professionally, none of them are in Manitoba. I know Gloria Grouse returned to school in the States. One name sticks in my mind but I can't tell exactly why. He's a grizzly bear named Grigor Gregory. He's a basso. I believe he left us under a bit of a cloud. A fight or something like that. I have no idea where he may be now or what he's doing. He may not be singing anymore. If you are dropped from a company for cause, that could spell curtains for your career. We have enough 'personalities' without taking on troublemakers. The other three don't ring any bells at all. Two rose-breasted grosbeaks *(they have lovely mezzo-soprano voices)* and a chipmunk who played character parts."

The Frau sighed, "Danke, Herr Professor. It was a bit of a long shot. Herr Maury, shall we go? Perhaps we should look in on the rehearsal hall."

After we left the Director's office, I turned to the Frau and said, "I don't know why but that bear named Gregory is making my nose twitch. How about you?"

She replied, "He's the only one of her former protégés big enough to kill her off. I can't see a chipmunk or a couple of birds doing that kind of damage. I'd like to know more about him but I'm not sure how to go about it. Perhaps the police can help. We'll be seeing the Sergeant this evening and could ask him to do a lookup for us. Let's talk to Wyatt about it. It could be total dead end."

"Which reminds me. That story you told me about Bearyl sneaking back out on Monday night has me puzzled. You're sure the bell-dog had his story straight."

A nod.

"If I was a member of the RCUP and I knew about this, I would be putting Bearyl on my high probability persons of interest list. I'm reluctant to say anything to anybody until we talk further with Octavius."

"Do you have any idea where Herr Bear is?"

"I think he's back at the hotel burning up cell towers and satellites running United Ursine and also checking on Belinda in the Shetlands."

We entered the rehearsal room. Lepi was doing a solo. Bearnice was sitting next to the Orchestra Leader, listening and nodding. Wyatt was lying down in the back of the room and Bearyl…where the hell was Bearyl?

Chapter Ten

Mid Wednesday Morning –CWP-TV Studios

Let's switch now to the latest TV.
All the news placed before you and me.
Want a murder or two?
Just remember that you
Saw it first on CWP!

Otto the Magnificent and L. Condor approached the security desk at CWP-TV. Condo stretched his twelve foot wings *(probably not the best thing to do under the circumstances)* handed the receptionist a business card and asked to see the station manager. Otto skittered up from behind the bird and did the same thing.

"May I tell Mr. Wapiti what this is aboot?"

"Certainly! Mr. Condor and I are assisting the RCUP in their investigations into the untimely death of Madame Honoria Heifer in the alley behind this station. We are both associates of Dr. Octavius Bear, the world famous detective, industrialist and electronics expert. I imagine some of your equipment originated in the labs of United Ursine Industries, his wholly owned high-tech enterprise. Please feel free to call Superintendent Caballus at the RCUP to confirm our credentials."

"I'll let Mister Wapiti make that determination. Please wait while I see if he's available." She kept staring at Condo while she made her call.

The raccoon put down the phone and said, "Mr. Wapiti is just wrapping up a meeting. He'll be with you momentarily. Please sir, forgive me for staring but what kind of bird are you? I've never seen one like you before."

Condo replied, changing the artificially generated voice coming from a small device clipped to his long neck, "I'm not surprised, Miss. I'm an Andean Condor. We don't get this far north very often."

"Did you just change your voice?"

"Yes, I did *(this time with a clipped British accent.)* You see, Condors have no voice box. We can't utter a sound naturally. However, with the assistance of the electronic geniuses at United Ursine Industries, I developed this voice synthesizer you see and hear on my neck. One of the add-on tweaks we put in the device is the ability to change voices and also to project my voice. *(This last phrase came from across the room.)*

"How wonderful! Here comes Mr. Wapiti. You must show this to him. I bet he'll want to make a feature clip aboot you."

"Good morning, gentlebeasts. Wally Wapiti, manager of CWP-TV. Frieda tells me you are here aboot that horrible death on Monday night. Terrible thing and right here on our premises! I'm not quite sure what I can do to assist you. The police gave the place a thorough going over and questioned all of the staff who might have been around."

Otto spoke up. "We know that, Mr. Wapiti…"

"Please, call me Wally"

"Wally. As we told your receptionist, we are associates of the world-famous detective and multi-billionaire, Octavius Bear. Madame Heifer was in the employ of Doctor Bear's wife, the Bearoness Belinda Béarnaise Bruin Bear *(nee Black)* assisting Ms Bearnice Blanc and Mr. Leperello in preparing for their recitals at the Winnipeg Opera this weekend. We understand you will be taping the performance."

"We'll be there for both performances and will pick the best parts from each. Then we broadcast next month."

L. Condor interrupted using his Portuguese accent. "Wonderful! We knew Madame Honoria and thought we could bring two fresh pairs of eyes to the scene. We certainly don't wish to upset your operation in any way but there may be a few clues we can garner based on our knowledge of the victim, her personality and activities. If you wish to consult with the police before allowing us access, we would be happy to have you call Superintendent Caballus."

(Narrator's aside. Otto and Condo were taking a bit of a risk here. It wasn't clear whether Caballus would recognize their names as being part of Octavius' group and how willing he would be to have the police's steps retraced by "amateurs." They were also engaging in a bit of razzle-dazzle. Condo would be attracting all the attention, rare bird that he is, especially with his ingenious voice apparatus. Otto would actually be the prime investigator with his special teleporting and illusionist talents genetically induced in him by the malevolent Imperius Drake. More of this as we progress.)

"Not necessary, Mr. Otter…"

"Otto, please and my Andean colleague here prefers Condo over his formal name, L. Condor."

"Thanks! *(Paw, hoof and wing shakes.)* I've never met an Andean Condor before. As I understand it, you birds do not have voice boxes and can't utter a sound naturally. How are you doing that?"

"Doing what?" said Condo

"That. Oh, I get it. You're pulling my leg. Seriously, does that little device on your neck have anything to do with it?"

"It has everything to do with it. Together with the technologists at Octavius Bear's Universal Ursine Industries, I designed and fabricated a micro-electronic voice prosthetic that picks up the impulses in my cortex and converts them to intelligible sound."

"And very intelligent sound, it seems."

"Thank you. We weren't content to just let it go at a flat synthetic voice so we worked on transmitting emotions, reactions and other elements that you speech gifted folks naturally have. Then, the UUI geeks took it even one or two steps further. I can speak to you in thirty-five correctly accented languages. Of course, I have to learn the language first before we can synthesize it. I learn the words. The prosthetic learns the accent and speech characteristics. Then we turn on the hydro, hoser and off we go, eh?"

"The elk broke out laughing, *(actually bugling)* and said, "Spoken like a true Canadian. We have to do something with this. Are you up for doing an interview?"

"Sure," he said, *(falling back on a Mid West American twang)* but we are here to do a little investigating. *(This time the voice came from across the room.)* Sorry, just showing off."

"You can also throw your voice?"

"All part of the service!"

"Wait right here while I rustle up a producer and check to see if Beatrice Beaver is in the house. She will love you. The staff will go wild." he said as he strode back into his office.

Condo winked at Otto and said, "Well, that should make it easier for you to snoop around while I'm beguiling the broadcasters. He wasn't paying any attention to you at all."

Otto smiled and responded, "Otters aren't exactly news in Canada. I certainly don't want to give a demonstration of my 'Now you see me, now you don't routines.' Ouch! That's a line Imperius Drake always used when he filched something. OK, I'll wander off and see what I can discover. I'd love to find that blunt instrument that did Honoria in. The cops haven't found it yet, have they."

"I think we would have heard, if they had. Now pardon me. I must get ready for my close-up, Mr. DeMille."

Chapter Eleven

Wednesday Afternoon –Ratison Hotel

The Great Bear thinks that now is the time
For reports from the scene of the crime.
Both the singers still swear
That they never were there
But the cops think, as suspects, they're prime.

Maury again: Frau Schuylkill and I left the rehearsal and headed back to the hotel to confer with Octavius. When we reached his room, he had Forrest Fox with him and he was just finishing a phone conversation with the RCUP Superintendent.

Octavius filled us in: "The police are of the opinion that Honoria was intercepted as she left the TV studios and was killed in the alley next to the station. She had sustained multiple gashes, sufficient to draw blood but not enough to kill her. The blows to her head had cracked her skull in several places and caused her death. This was obviously the work of one or more strong individuals, equipped with massive claws and enough body mass to take down the heavy set cow. They have not yet found the weapon. The Medical Examiner believes she was already down when she was struck repeatedly."

"No witnesses have turned up as yet. An unlocked gate two meters high between two studio buildings closes in the well-lit alley. The gate should have been locked but has often been left open because of the heavy traffic that goes through and across the alley. One building houses the main studios. The other is storage for remote broadcast trucks and equipment. Several locked doors in each building lead out into the alley as well. Four large dumpsters line one wall. There was no sign of forced entry or exit on any of the doors. There had been no remote program activity overnight so the body remained untouched until the trash collectors came upon it. The Police have sorted through the dumpsters and have come up with several objects that might have been the murder weapon. They're being analyzed in the Crime Lab now."

"Well," I said, "Otto and L. Condor are at the studios and crime scene now. Let's see what, if anything, they come up with. Maybe you should call Otto on his cell phone and tell him what the Police told you."

"Good idea!" said the Bear. "Why don't you two work with Forrest here while I call. We need a plan for our bar search this evening."

Forrest and the two of us moved to the other room in the suite. Octavius roars when he's on the phone and no other conversation has a hope of surviving. Things suddenly went quiet and then a "thump." Oh boy, the Great Bear had just had one of his narcoleptic seizures. We'll have to wait him out. Hopefully, it will be a short one. Meanwhile we set about holding Forrest's attention. We didn't feel like giving him the short course on Octavius' condition.

The Frau and I had decided to keep the lawyer in the dark about Bearyl and our suspicions. We'll keep that in the family for the moment. No doubt he would love to use that to further advance his defense of Bearnice and

Lepi. If their story isn't corroborated by the folks at the bar tonight, that's the time to raise the Bearyl story.

The Frau looked over at the lawyer and asked, "Herr Fox, suppose we can't find this bar or suppose they don't back up the singers' stories, what do you think the police will do?"

"It all depends on what other evidence they come up with. I was hoping they'd locate the weapon. That could go a great way toward pointing to a possible culprit or culprits. But it would help a lot if we can demonstrate that they were somewhere else at the time of the killing."

I chimed in, "A good prosecutor could always cast doubt on the Medical Examiner's time of death estimate, I suppose, but without any other supporting evidence to prove they were at the crime scene, that shouldn't be enough."

The Fox frowned, "Right now, I'm only interested in keeping them out of court, period. Do you think your two associates will come up with anything at the TV station?"

"Well, I'll share one piece of information with you that we don't want to go any further. Otto can get through locked doors and into secure areas. If there's something there, he'll probably find it."

"He picks locks?"

"Not really. He just ignores them. It's a very unique talent."

"I don't understand."

"Most animals don't, including us. As they say, 'It is what it is.' We just use the results. He does quite an illusionist's act with the Aquabears, by the way. He's my client, too. I'm also the theatrical agent for the polar twins, Lepi and Otto. The Aquabears are thinking of signing on but that will have to wait until the Bearoness comes out of her pre-natal hibernation. She owns the review. You'll have to meet her. I'm sure she'd welcome you to her castle-resort. She'll be very thankful for your assistance in this case. I don't suppose you're licensed to practice in Scotland."

"Not me personally but several members of our firm are. They handle all sorts of international business affairs, personal liability and such but we steer away from foreign criminal cases and of course, crime is my specialty."

"I'm off the phone," roared Octavius. His outage had been extremely short.

As we filed back into the large bedroom, Octavius said, "I briefed Otto. It seems L. Condor got waylaid into giving the TV folks an interview aboot *(Him too!)* his voice device. He has the whole station lining up to see and hear a demonstration. Not bad publicity for UUI. It also allows Otto to move around more freely. Not that he needs much assistance. So what's our plan?"

"I'm sorry," said Forrest. "We got sidetracked but I do have one idea. Before the police sergeant shows up and before we have dinner, why don't I go out with Lepi and see if we can find the bar. That way we can get right to it after we eat without any unnecessary missteps. If we can't find it, we'll have time to work up another story."

"Sounds good. I wonder if this hotel stocks mead in the bar. I'd like to talk to that bartender myself."

"If they don't, I smuggled in a few kegs on the Ursa Major, Herr Bear. They are in my room."

"Frau, you are indeed a wonder. Always anticipating. Thank you."

I looked over at a rather puzzled Forrest Fox and said, "You should know that Octavius breeds bees and distills some of the finest mead in the world. He has won major awards. In addition to her other specialties, Frau Schuylkill is also a cordon bleu chef. She too has won many awards."

The wolf blushed. *(A rare sight.)* While she and Octavius went off in search of the freight elevator, Forrest and I took the normal size car to the ground floor and the lobby bar. The same bobcat was on duty and recognized me. "How's your wounded ear?" he asked, "You got tossed aboot a bit the other night."

"No major damage. It comes with the territory. Actually, I'd like you to meet my boss, Dr. Octavius Bear. He'll be here in a minute. He had to take the freight elevator. You'll soon see why."

As I said this, the Great Bear trundled into the lounge with the wolf in tow. The bartender gaped as Octavius stood on his hind legs stretching to his full nine foot *(2.7432 meters)* height. It always worked. "Good afternoon. Is it possible you might stock mead among your wares?" he asked.

"Yessir, I think we have a bottle of Old BuzzBee's Reserve. I'll search it out."

"Not a great brand but it'll have to do" muttered Octavius as the bobcat ran off. "Is he the one who was on duty the night of the "event?"

"Yeah, he's the one who gave me the napkins to stop my ear's bleeding. He's also the one who gave evidence to the Police."

The bartender returned, poured out a healthy swig into a bowl and placed it before the Bear. Octavius sniffed, twirled the bowl and lapped up a small taste. His nose wrinkled and his eyes almost shut. "I'm afraid this bottle has gone bad. Probably been around too long. Do you have another?"

"Sorry, sir. That's all we have."

"OK. I'll make up my mind on something else while you three order. A little pre-dinner aperitif, even if it's only 3 o'clock. Plenty of time for lots of other things to go wrong."

He turned and stared out at the lobby, not believing his eyes. Sauntering across the floor behind a bell-dog, the last animal he ever wanted to see was approaching the lounge. Handing her key to the dog along with a substantial tip, she told him to leave her things in the room and return with her key. Then she turned, entered the bar, winked at the Frau and me and said, "Hi Octavius! Missed me?"

Chita

Chita Had Arrived !

Chapter Twelve

Wednesday Afternoon –The Century Concert Hall

Though their lives are a heck of a mess,
Their rehearsals are quite a success.
But there's serious doubt.
They can't quite figure out
Whether Bearyl did try on that dress.

"Brava! Bravo!" shouted Hartley, the Opera's Orchestra Leader, "very well done. I don't think I've ever had a rehearsal go so smoothly and flawlessly before."

Bearnice curtsied and Lepi bowed, both with beaming smiles. *(Of course when a Polar Bear and a Himalayan Snow Leopard smile, they can look pretty threatening with all those teeth.)*

Wyatt, who had been stretched out in the back of the rehearsal hall got to his feet and vehemently clapped his front paws. He walked up to front of the room and patted each of the soloists on the back and shook Hartley's paw. "Well done, Maestro and you too, Ms…er."

He meant the accompanist who was still sitting at the piano. A mountain goat with a frizzy hairdo, she peered at the wolf and said, "Thank you, we seldom get any credit for a fine performance. The name is Giselle, by the way."

"Well you certainly deserve credit, Giselle. What's next, Maestro?"

"I think we can call it a day. You two have worked very hard and deserve some down time. I think we're ready to go to the stage tomorrow and then Friday we'll work with the full orchestra."

"Wonderful," said Bearnice. "I hate to say it but things went so much better without Honoria here, interrupting, criticizing and making her ridiculous suggestions. She was a real trial. I certainly didn't want to see her dead, especially so horribly, but one way or the other, she had to be taken out of the picture."

The Colonel looked at her and said, "You may want to choose your words a little more carefully, Bearnice." He looked over at Hartley and Giselle who said nothing.

Suddenly, the door to the rehearsal room opened and Bearyl padded in. "Oh, are you wrapping up? I thought you'd still be at it."

"No," said Hartley. "We finished in record time and record style. Mr. Leperello and your sister are true professionals."

"Yeah, in spite of what Honoria thought." Murmured Lepi as he collected their music and tote bags.

"Well, Giselle and I will see you tomorrow on the main stage at ten o'clock. We can rehearse entrances and exits and you can get used to the auditorium acoustics and sight lines. We don't want you walking out of the audience's view. We'll do a complete run-through, non-stop. We need to time the performance for the orchestra's use at Friday's dress rehearsal. Also on Friday, the TV people will be in the house plotting out their set-ups so you'll have to contend with that. We'll need to time that performance more carefully. It's going to be a tough couple of days but I'm sure you two are up to it."

"Thank you so much, Hartley and you too, Giselle. You've been wonderful to work with. We'll be ready." This from Bearnice.

The colonel turned to Bearyl. "Welcome back. May I ask where you've been?"

"Oh, er, I was down in the wardrobe department checking out Bearnice's costumes."

Wyatt cocked his head. "I thought Frau Ilse was taking care of that."

"She is. At least she's paying for them and making sure they're completed on time. I just thought that since Bearnice and I are identical, I'd try them on and see how they looked."

"So, how do they look?" asked her twin.

"Oh, wonderful! I especially liked the white one with the large red maple leaf."

Lepi piped up. "Are we all ready to leave?"

Bearyl led the procession out of the rehearsal room, down the hall and out through the lobby. Lepi followed. Bearnice reached out to the colonel and pulled him back a few steps.

"Something strange! Talk to the Frau. I thought we cancelled that maple leaf dress on Monday."

Chapter Thirteen

Wednesday Afternoon – CWP-TV Studios

Condo offers a voice demonstration.
Otto starts an in-depth exploration.
After snooping around,
What he found will astound
It's the weapon! Ain't that a sensation?

Condo had a captive audience. Wally Wapiti had dragooned a production crew into one their larger studios and was getting Beatrice Beaver *(Yes, that Beatrice Beaver!)* brought up to speed on the fabulous condor. A number of the staff had crowded into the rear of the room while the cameras, lights and chairs were being adjusted. Right now, CWP was taking a network feed from the CBC so with exception of a couple of engineers, everyone else had abandoned their posts to see the unique bird.

Otto was standing in the back, chuckling to himself. They had actually staged an impromptu lineup of possible suspects. From the stage, Condo scanned the room, looking for animals who might have had the size, strength and mobility to have killed the cow. There weren't many, if you believed it was a solo effort. Two or more perpetrators would change the calculus but somehow they both believed it was carried out by a single individual. A couple of large wildcats, a bear handling a mike boom, a ram, two caribou and that was it. Of course, there was also Wally Wapiti but like the caribou and ram, he didn't have claws and the police believed the cow's wounds were caused by claws or claw-like instruments.

Otto skittered to the studio door, stepped out in the hallway, looked both ways and zapped down to the remote vehicle garage on one side of the crime-scene alley. Several trucks were lined up in the large room. Four auxiliary generators took up a lot of space and what looked like replacement satellite dishes were spread out on heavy duty tables. The rest of the room was taken up with workstations, tool boxes, closets and what looked liked a generous supply of spare parts. The station's broadcast antennas must have been somewhere off site.

A door opened on the alley side of the building and a female Arctic Fox slipped in and walked to one of the work tables. She was carrying a laptop device that she placed on the table surface and connected it to a workstation. Otto slipped around the truck he had been sitting on and watched, ready to disappear if she looked his way. She seemed to be entering tables of numbers and letters. When she finished, she walked over to a closet, opened a combination lock and slipped the device onto a shelf. Almost buried, far below the shelf was something that caught the otter's enhanced eyes. A large wrench that didn't seem to match the rest of the closet's contents. Electronics, spare keyboards, printer paper and ink, CDs, thumb drives and…a large wrench. When she closed the door, he peered at the closet label. Computer supplies.

He waited for the fox to leave, ran over to the closet, went through his combination lock foiling routine, opened the door and taking a pair of gloves from one of the work benches, eased the wrench out of the pile of paper it was under. There were stains on its head. Looked like blood but he couldn't be

85

sure. He put the tool back in the closet, closed the door but changed the combination on the lock. He took out his cell phone and called Octavius. They needed to turn it over to the police but they didn't want to tell them how Otto had found it. A conundrum.

Back in the studio, Condo had just switched back to his Latin Lover basso for the third time to the intense laughter of his audience after exactly mimicking Beatrice Beaver's voice right down to the last lisp. Otto re-appeared at the back of the room and none too subtly signaled to the Condor to cut it short. Condo flapped his huge wings and said, "Ms Beaver, this has been delightful but my companion and I are late for a very important appointment. So I must say *obrigada* and *boa tarde*."

Bowing to the applause and whistles, he flapped his wings and left the stage. As they worked their way out of the crowded room, Wally Wapiti came up to them and said, "Thanks so much. Are you staying at the Ratison? I'll send over a DVD of the interview and we'll let you know when we broadcast it."

"That would be wonderful, Wally. I wonder if we could speak to Beatrice for a moment."

The manager waved at Beatrice and she skittered over to them. "Yesh, Mr. Condor?"

"Please call me Condo and this is my associate, Otto." *(He deliberately left off the "Magnificent" or Otto would have been next up for an interview and demonstration. Something not to be desired at the moment.)* We are actually here assisting the police in their search for the killers of Madame Honoria Heifer and were wondering if you could shed further light on her itinerary after she finished your live interview the other night."

"I'm sho shorry, Condo and Otto, but ash shoon as she finished her interview, she left with a production asshishtant asshigned to her. I'm not sure where she went."

"Can you tell us who the assistant was?" asked Otto.

"Oh, yesh. It was Felicia. She's my personal asshishtant. Shall I get her for you?"

"I'm afraid we don't have time at the moment but we would like to talk to her tomorrow. Can you arrange that?"

"Of courshe."

"I assume both of you were interviewed by the police."

"I wash. I don't know aboot Felicia. I would asshume sho."

"Thanks again Beatrice. We'll call you tomorrow."

While this conversation was going on, they had worked their way out into the lobby and hailed a cab. Condo turned to Otto and asked, "What's so important that we had to rush out of there. I was really beginning to enjoy myself."

"I think I found the murder weapon and Octavius is waiting for us."

Chapter Fourteen

Later Wednesday Afternoon – The Ratison Bar

For our hero, The Great Kodiak
Things are turning a deep shade of black.
It's been tough all day long.
How much more could go wrong?
Quite a lot! Hey, Ms Chita is back!

Octavius looked down at Chita and said, "I suppose I should have expected you. You can't seem to stay away from trouble."

"What trouble? I'm just here with my photographer to cover the Great Canadian Recital for *PURR* and *SOW* magazines. The first editions featuring the Edinbeargh recital were sell-outs. Of course, the Lion and the Unicorn helped. *(cf. Volume Three -The Case of Scotch)* But our readers want more of Lepi and Bearnice. *(Notice, the cat came first.)* I would have sent a staff writer but seeing as how it's my old singing partner Lepi along with Bearnice, I thought I'd cover it myself. By the by, my nom de plume is Madame Catherine Catt."

Madame?!

You seem to forget I was briefly mated to Pontius Puma, the bastard!

"So you've taken over Da Savile Row Publications?"

"Well, Bearbi and her son are facing charges of attempted murder of the Bearoness. She'll be in court as soon as she recovers from her fall. I am the junior partner, so for the time being at least, I'm *numero uno*. It'll all sort itself out but what's this trouble you're talking about?"

"Honoria Heifer has been murdered!"

"These kids are two-for-two! They can't have a recital without a killing being tossed in the mix. Wow, that's going to goose up the story. Tell all, tell all!"

Octavius phone rang. Otto!

"Maury," he said, "introduce Madame Catt to Forrest and then you and the Frau can bring our spotted "friend" up to speed. I have to take this call."

Bowls of champagne suddenly appeared. So did a bowl of fermented coconut milk VSOP for me. I noticed that Octavius had a small keg of mead by his side. Frau Schuylkill had the bar and bartender under control and had made it back to her room to retrieve the mead. I winked at her. "Hyperspeed again?"

"Ja, but those verdammt elevators are so slow."

Octavius was talking, quietly if you can believe it, with Otto while all this was going on. "Yes, I understand. You and Condo hurry on back here. Are you sure the closet is secure? Fine. Well, there's nothing for it. We'll have to demonstrate what you can do just the way we did in the Shetlands with Superintendent Wardlaw. In fact, after we meet with Superintendent Caballus,

I may ask him to call Shetland Yard for corroboration. We don't want to be accused of tampering with or withholding evidence. By the way, good job, both of you. Any thoughts on who the culprit might be? OK, we can discuss it when you get here."

The Frau and I were just about wrapping up our Chita (Sorry! Madame Catherine Catt's) briefing. Forrest kept staring at the cat in stupefaction. I wonder what his reaction would have been if he knew her complete history. He's not going to hear it from us.

Out in the lobby, Bearnice, Lepi and the colonel were striding in. The two singers were looking very self-satisfied. Bearyl had peeled off and was heading for the elevators as the others spotted us in the bar. "Spotted" is exactly right. Lepi saw Chita and bounded over to her. "Hey, amiga, good to see you!" They hugged.

Bearnice extended her paw to the cat. They did not hug. The colonel nodded in Chita's direction but said nothing.

While Madame Catt explained her plans for covering the recital to Bearnice and Lepi, the Colonel joined the Frau and me. "The rehearsal went beautifully," he said, "they are real professionals. I need to ask you about the costumes."

Frau Ilse looked at him quizzically. "What about them? Is there something wrong? They were delivered to the Center's wardrobe department on Monday and I paid for them. Bearnice hasn't had a chance to try them on as far as I know."

"Yes, but Bearyl claims she did. She Bearnice's exact size. She especially liked the one with the big red maple leaf."

"Ach, we cancelled that one. We didn't think it was respectful of Canada's flag."

"You might want to check. Bearnice thinks it was canceled, too."

The Frau already had her cell phone out and was calling the wardrobe department. "Hello, this is Frau Ilse Schuylkill with the weekend recital group. Yes, I remember you, too. I have a question. Do you recall Bearnice Blanc's dress with the big red maple leaf? It _was_ cancelled! That's strange. The soloist's twin sister Bearyl said she was in your department today and tried the dress on. No one came by? All day? Were you there the whole time? Ja! Well, danke. No, no trouble. I'm sure Bearnice will be by tomorrow early. The dress rehearsal is on Friday and we need to give you time for any alterations. Ja, Good-bye."

The wolves stared at each other. Wyatt broke the silence. "What the hell is Bearyl playing at?"

"I don't know but I intend to find out."

"Does she realize she appears awfully suspicious? I don't believe she had anything to do with the heifer's death but if the police hear from the bell-dog, they may think otherwise."

Just then Octavius called them over and said to the colonel. "I'd like you to take Lepi, Maury and Forrest out for a ride around the area right now.

Let's see if you can find that bar they claim they were in before the RCUP sergeant shows up. It'll look a lot more credible if we can take him right to the spot without any searching around. If you can't find it, we'll need another game plan."

Lepi said goodbye to Chita and Bearnice and walked with Wyatt, Forrest and me to the valet parking desk. The wolves had brought an ATV with them on the Ursa Major.

Reluctantly, Octavius invited Madame Catherine to join them for dinner at six. *(It was now four-thirty.)* Otherwise, she'd be sticking her nose into everything in sight. Oh hell, she would anyway. She headed off to the lobby lounge to call up her photographer who was coming in on a plane early next morning.

Otto and Condo arrived. They waved at us at the valet desk and then Otto spotted Chita. He broke away from Condo and ran over to say hello. It was Meet and Greet time in the Ratison lobby. Octavius called him back over. "Time for that later," he roared. "Let's go up to my rooms"

The valet brought the car. Otto, Condo and Octavius headed for the elevators, Frau Schuylkill went off looking for Bearyl. Bearnice had already left for their room. Silence settled over a solitary spotted cat murmuring into her cell phone and wondering if she wanted to have dinner with a Canadian Police Sergeant. What the hell, she was incognito and she wasn't doing anything important, anyway.

Chapter Fifteen

Later Wednesday Afternoon – The Streets of Winnipeg

We need proof of exact where and when.
Here's that neighborhood bar once again.
Where we hope they'll agree
That they really did see
Our two singers on Monday at ten.

Wyatt was driving. Lepi was riding shotgun up front while Forrest and I took up the back seats.

"Do you remember from which direction you approached the hotel on your way back?" asked the Colonel.

"I vaguely remember passing that big church so it must have been out that way. It can't be far. We were too worn out to have been gallivanting around."

"Did you have rough idea where the hotel was when you started back?'

"I think we asked directions from someone in the bar."

"Any of it coming back to you?"

"No, I don't think they gave us street names. I think it's off Main Street."

"So is everything."

"Wait a second. Drive around the block. This looks familiar,"

"You would pick a street that has one, two, three, six bars and taverns."

"Give me a second. The place had a cutesy name and the owner was a female Canada Lynx. So was the bartender. I think they were mates. It's coming back."

"There's the Portage Pub"

"Nah!"

"Winnie-the-Pooh?"

"Too cutesy!"

"Kitty's Kozy Korner?"

"Bingo! That's it. Are they open?"

"Looks like. Let me find a place to park."

After a few fruitless runs up and down the street, we found a municipal parking garage and pulled in.

I piped up from the back seat. "I don't think we should all go in. Why don't I go in with Lepi and we'll see if we can strike up a conversation. You two will probably be coming back with the police sergeant later on. We don't want to get the natives all nervous."

Wyatt looked skeptical but agreed. Forrest just told us to play it cool. If Maury Meerkat is anything, he is cool and Lepi, well, Lepi is Lepi.

The place had a fair size clientele. Aha, Happy Hour! Music in the background. Conversations, high pitched laughter, a guffaw or two. Sure enough, two Canada Lynx *(Lynxes?)* were behind the bar.

"Hi gentlebeasts, what'll you have. It's Happy Hour. Two for the price of one. "Hey, wait a second," she exclaimed, looking at me, "I remember you."

Not the answer we wanted. Then it dawned. She was cross-eyed and was really looking at Lepi.

"You were in here the other night with some polar bear floozie. We get our share of those kind in here but I don't ever remember ever seeing any cat like you before. You said you were a Himalayan Snow Leopard, right?"

"That's right and I'm his friend, an African Meerkat. Bet you don't see many of us either." I was trying frantically to keep Lepi from reacting to the "floozie" remark.

"Nope, can't say that I do but you're just a little pipsqueak compared to this gorgeous hunk. You had half the females in the place slobbering all over themselves the other night. What's your name, honey?"

"Lepi, short for leopard. Do you remember when I was in here?"

"Sure, and if I don't there are plenty of other females who do. It was Monday. You and that polar lollapalooza came in here looking all tired out, ordered a couple of drinks and sat over there in the corner. Every cat in the place strolled past your table in the couple of hours you sat there."

"Do you remember the time, exactly?'

"Well, I remember the hockey game was going into its final period when you walked in. The Jets were winning for a change. Oh, aboot nine thirty or so."

"And when did they leave?

"Oh, not for good while. Hour, hour and a half. Hey, shorty, what's this all aboot?"

Lepi jumped in. "Look, we're going to need your help. In a few hours, we're going to be coming back here with a member of the RCUP."

"Hey, I don't want any trouble with the police."

"You're not in trouble. I _am_ and you can get me out of trouble if you're willing. The cops are trying to pin a crime on me and my polar friend that happened at ten o'clock Monday on the other side of town. I need you and some of your customers to tell them the truth. At ten o'clock, I was sitting here finishing off my second or third Scotch. I even remember the hockey match. The Jets did win."

"Who are you, really?"

"The Polar bear and I are singers. We've giving recitals at the Winnipeg Opera on Saturday and Sunday. Our voice coach got killed on Monday night and the Police think we may have had something to do with it. We didn't and you can help us prove it."

"I saw that on the telly. She was a cow, right? Wow, now that's something to think aboot. Hey, my mate and I love opera. Big fans! OK, bring in the cop. Can he come in plain clothes? I guess it won't matter much if we're going to let him talk to some of the regulars but let's not shake up the shopping crowd."

"Lepi grabbed her paws and said, "We'll be back and we'll bring front seat tickets for the concert."

"Hold it," I squeaked, "I'll bring them by tomorrow. We don't want the cops to think we're bribing you."

"Gotcha, Shorty. See you later. Bring your polar friend. Opera stars in Kitty's Kozy Korner. Who'd a thunk?"

Chapter Sixteen

Later Wednesday Afternoon-Ratison Hotel

Otto has a formidable trick
That we all think is really quite slick.
He can go any place
Without leaving a trace
And just zap back again, super quick.

Octavius, Otto and Condo settled down in the suite and the Great Bear turned to Otto. "So you think that wrench may be the murder weapon."

"It has stains on the head that look like blood but the police will have to analyze it."

"OK, I'm going to call the Superintendent and ask him to join us. Before we tell him your story, you're going to have to do an after dinner demonstration of your powers just like you did for Superintendent Wardlaw in the Shetlands. That should take the edge off any thoughts he may have about accusing you of tampering with evidence."

"Well, it's no secret, really, especially if I'm going to appear as an illusionist with the Aquabear Revue. I'd prefer to keep quiet about how I got this way, particularly since I don't know exactly how I did get this way. Are Drs. Vark and BingBang any closer to a solution? I'm still scared stiff that I'm going to turn into a nut job after all those injections Imperius Drake gave me."

"We've only been away from UUI for a couple of days and the doctors have been working the lab overtime on sorting out your genes and DNA. If they have any kind of a breakthrough, you'll be the first to know. We do know that your "gifts" surface with a rise in your adrenalin."

"Gifts!? Yeah, well maybe, but if the price of being a matinee idol is going crazy in the process, I'd be just as happy to head back to my family on the St. Lawrence and forget the whole thing."

"You may not be able to forget the whole thing. Look, I promised we would spare no effort in getting to the bottom of Imperius' chicanery and we will. If it turns out he's done you some permanent damage, we'll do everything we can to help work around it. In the meantime, you might as well use the effects to your and our advantage."

"I suppose so. Are you inviting the Superintendent to dinner? We already have that Sergeant coming to check out Lepi's and Bearnice's story."

"Condo laughed, "This is turning into a mob scene complete with the cops."

"I'm about to call the Super. Anything else I should know before I talk to him?"

"When I was doing my party piece for the TV cameras," said Condo, "most of the station staff showed up to watch the proceedings. That gave us a chance to see how many of them looked capable of killing off Honoria. There weren't many. Let's see: Two large wildcats, a bear, a ram, two caribou and a partridge in a pear tree. *(Kidding!)* That was it, wasn't it, Otto?"

100

Nod!

"There's also the Wapiti station manager, but like the caribou and ram, he didn't have claws and the Police think the cow's wounds were caused by claws or claw-like instruments. By the way, Otto and I will be making a return visit in the morning to talk with Beatrice Beaver's personal assistant. She escorted Honoria out of the studios. I suppose the police talked to her but it won't hurt for us to follow up."

"Good. That may give us a few more pieces for the puzzle."

"I think we already have too many pieces, Octavius" Otto complained. "It would be nice if a few of them fit together."

"Welcome to the wonderful world of detection, Otto. That's what makes it such a challenge. OK, I'm going to call the Super now. Stand by in case he has any questions I can't answer."

"Rowan? Octavius Bear here. We have something that might be of interest to you but we have to show you in person. Can you meet us at say, eight o'clock, outside the CWP studios? By yourself, please. I'll explain it all when we meet. No, I am not being deliberately mysterious. It's just not something I can explain adequately over the phone. Is your sergeant still set to accompany the singers to the bar they were in on Monday night? I think that will clear up a few things, He's been invited to dinner with us at six here at the hotel. So are you, if you have the time. No? OK, then eight it is at CWP. Thanks. Anything new on your end? None of the potential weapons your squad took in for testing paid off. Interesting! Well, see you at eight."

He turned to Otto and Condo. "You heard that? Makes it all the more likely that the wrench you uncovered could be what the police are looking for. I want both of you to come with me tonight. You do your illusionist's thing, Otto and you, Senhor Condor, can share your thoughts on possible CWP involvement. Now, let's get ready for dinner."

He turned and slowly slipped to the floor. Narcolepsy time! Out for the count. Otto and Condo silently slipped out the door.

Chapter Seventeen

5:30 PM -Ratison Hotel

Chita's lapping a bowl of champagne.
Bearyl Blanc has gone missing again.
And to light up our lives,
Sergeant Preston arrives
And turns out to be really a pain.

Madame Catherine was once again sitting alone at the Ratison Bar, lapping at *(what else?)* a bowl of the Hotel's best champagne which really wasn't all that great. "Oh well," she thought, "knowing Octavius, he probably flew in some Grande Marque vintage courtesy of Frau Schuylkill especially for dinner. I've got to get in sync with that she wolf. The Bearoness and I get along well, in spite of my spotted past. Octavius is such a self-righteous stiff that I doubt we'll ever be comfortable with each other. I love Otto and Maury. But that wolf, actually both those wolves, can be formidable opponents and at the same time very powerful allies. I'm going to have to work on them while I'm here. Who knows?"

Just then a long furry tail wrapped itself around her shoulders. "Hey Amiga, how ya doin?" Lepi! Along with the Colonel, Forrest Fox and me. *(Maury! Remember?)* "We need to catch up. I'm going back out after dinner with Bearnice, Forrest and the Unmountie Sergeant to that bar we were in on Monday. I was there this afternoon. They remembered us. I hope that pulls us out of the Suspects' Corner and lets us settle in on our recitals. But if you're

103

still around when we come back, we can have a drink and get back up to speed. I understand you're an oil tycoon and a publishing magnate. Beats singing in beer joints in Rio. I heard Pontius Puma is in the tank. That guy was the scourge of all Brazil plus quite a few other places. Sorry, have I touched a nerve?"

"Not really," said the cat, "He was a cheating bastard. I've filed for divorce. We were registered mates, probably along with a long procession of other tootsies. Polygamous Pontius! Anyway, I'll see you at dinner. You too, Short Stuff. Nice meeting you, Mr. Fox. You don't happen to handle Brazilian divorces, do you?"

"Sorry, ma'am. I'm a criminal defense lawyer and it sounds like you don't want this Puma person defended."

"God, no! He's in a U.S. jail at the moment and I hope he rots there. Anyway. See you at dinner where we can keep the conversation more pleasant."

*****

Dinner began promptly at six. Octavius wouldn't have it any other way. We gathered in a conference room on the mezzanine floor.

Let's call the roll: Octavius, Lepi, Bearnice, The Frau, Colonel Where, Otto, Condo, Forrest Fox, Madame Catherine and me. Wait a second! Where the hell was Bearyl? Missing in action again! I looked over at Frau Schuylkill and mouthed, "Where's Bearyl?"

She shrugged and then frowned. Something screwy going on. Bearyl couldn't be evading the police, could she? Nah!

The RCUP Sergeant had arrived *(A Husky. Sergeant Preston, if you can believe it.)* and was being a bit of trial. *(No pun intended. Aw, hell! Yes, it was intended.)*

"Now you understand, Dr. Bear, that my having dinner with you will in no way influence my judgment aboot the evidence we may gather this evening. I am somewhat suspicious aboot the fact that at least one of the suspects and several others went out to the bar this afternoon and talked to the owner."

Forrest Fox was on it immediately. "If you want to ask the owner and patrons of the establishment to swear under oath aboot the whereaboots of Mr. Leperello and Ms Blanc on Monday evening during the time of the murder, I am certain that those honest citizens would be happy to comply. A bit heavy-handed, I would think, Sergeant. You may wish to check with Superintendent Caballus before you do. You may also be casting aspersions on the integrity of Mr. Meerkat, Colonel Where and myself, all of whom have a history of successfully and honestly assisting law enforcement in a wide range of criminal cases."

The dog harrumphed several times and mumbled, "I will do my duty as I see it." He then proceeded to slurp his bowl of pea soup getting spots of green on his shaggy muzzle and napkin. Somehow his bright red uniform remained unsullied. So much for asking him to come in plain clothes. He had a marked police car, too. Kitty will not be pleased.

Lepi had not had a chance to bring Bearnice up to speed on the afternoon's events at the bar and was quietly enlightening her, leaving out references to *"polar tootsies"* and *"lollapaloozas."*

Otto, Condo and Octavius said nothing about Otto's discovery or their appointment with the Superintendent later this evening. I would have loved to be there when the Super saw Otto in action but I felt I had to stay with the bar hoppers and support the team.

Chita was chatting up Forrest. Probably cementing relations in case she ever needed representation by criminal counsel in Canada. Knowing her likely rap sheet from her days with Imperius Drake and her solo acts afterward, she could probably use criminal counsel anywhere in the world. Her Catherine Catt pseudonym was, no doubt, intended to shroud her true identity. Flimsy but what the hell. I still liked her, much to Octavius' disgust.

The conversation then shifted to the singers' performance today and their schedule for the rest of the week, Sergeant Preston notwithstanding. The Colonel repeated the Orchestra Leader's ecstatic reaction. No one had the bad taste to mention Honoria's absence as a positive influence on their progress.

Promptly at seven, we finished our meal. *(The Sergeant had two desserts.)* He wanted Lepi and Forrest to ride with him in the police car. Bearnice and I took a cab. Octavius stayed behind to further strategize Otto's performance and Condo's opinions for the Superintendent at CWP at eight. The Colonel would be joining them and driving them to the TV station. The Frau decided to stay back as well, starting a one animal wolf pack search for Bearyl. I'm not sure where Madame Catt went.

Chapter Eighteen

7:15 PM –Kitty's Kozy Korner

Kitty's patrons came through like real champs,
Giving Preston a bad case of cramps.
They swore snow cat and bear
Monday night were both there
And then sealed it with notary stamps.

"Oh Gawd, Maxie! Look who's shambling through the door in his robust red finery. It's Prissy Preston of the RCUP." This was Kitty talking to her husband-partner. "He's with that scrumptious leopard and a fox I don't recognize. I wonder where the little meerkat and the Polar Bear opera singer are. They were supposed to come, too. Imagine me mistaking her for a tootsie. Oh, here they come now. Make sure the clientele stick around. Tell them we've extended Happy Hour."

Maxie circulated around the tables and bar stools spreading the Happy Hour News and explaining why the police were there. "Nothing wrong with us! We're just confirming the fact that the Himalayan Snow Leopard and his Polar Bear partner were here on Monday night around ten. They're classical singers and they're giving recitals this weekend at the Winnipeg Opera. Seems their voice coach got herself killed Monday night aboot ten o'clock over near CWP's studios. The cops seem to think the singers might have done for her but they were here, all the way across town from the crime scene. Seems the

RCUP want a sworn statement from Kitty and me and anyone else who remembers seeing them here that night."

Several customers raised their paws or hooves and allowed as how it would be pretty tough to forget a really hot snow leopard (this from the females) and a gorgeous polar beauty (the males) and sure, they remembered them.

Sergeant Preston was standing at the bar making official noises and trying to look Kitty in the eye. Being cross-eyed, the Canada Lynx was talking to the dog but looking at Forrest Fox who had just introduced himself. Bearnice came up to the rail and said hello to Kitty. Now the cop was really confused at how the conversation was going and tried to get a word or two in edgewise along with a few "harrumphs."

I interrupted. "Miss Kitty, I think we can get this all over with very quickly and let you and your patrons get back to some serious drinking. I think you remember me. I'm Maury Meerkat, theatrical agent, and I represent Ms Bearnice Blanc and Mr. Leperello. Mr. Fox here is their attorney. Can you or can't you tell us whether they were in your establishment on Monday night around ten o'clock?"

Preston started to speak but Kitty interrupted. "Of course, they were here. Who could forget them? Does this place look like somewhere a drop-dead Polar beauty and a matinee idol Snow Leopard could come and not be remembered? Some of our regulars were here that night. Do any of you folks remember seeing these two on Monday night aboot ten o'clock?"

Shouts of "Sure, you bet, who could forget?"

Preston finally got to speak. "I shall have to get sworn statements to that effect. I have here a document stating that Ms Blanc and Mr. Leperello were on these premises Monday night at or aboot ten o'clock and did not leave until close to eleven. Would you care to look at this, Mr. Fox?"

Forrest growled at the policeman. "This is all so damned unnecessary, Sergeant but very well, let's get this stupid mess cleared up. I don't see anything wrong with the statement. Ms Kitty and Maxie, you can feel free to sign if you honestly believe the statement to be true and any of you other folks can too, if you wish."

The volunteers lined up. Twelve signatures in all.

Preston growled back at Forrest. "Of course, I shall have to get this notarized."

A red deer sitting in the back popped up her head and said, "I'll do it. I didn't sign so I can notarize it. I always carry my seal with me." Sure enough, sitting next to her was a Canadian Harp Seal. *(Sorry, I couldn't resist.)* She reached in her bag, came forward and notarized the document.

Kitty was standing behind Preston and stuck her tongue out at him, causing peals of laughter at the unsuspecting dog's expense. "Tell you what, Preston. I'll even make copies for everyone involved. On the house! While I'm doing that, would you two do us all a favor and sing something for us?"

"Sure, we'd love to." Said Lepi. "A cappella, of course. How about a song made famous by that celebrated Canadian duo, Jennet McDonkey and Nelson Eagle. The Indian Love Howl?"

Applause and shouts from the patrons. Sighs of relief and laughter from the team.

Kitty came back with the copies. Sergeant Preston picked up his signed original of the statement, stomped through the door and out to his car as two melodious voices entwined:

"When I'm calling you-oo-oo oo-oo-oo!

 Will you answer too-oo-oo oo-oo-oo?"

(Oh, well, I guess we'll all have to take a cab back to the hotel.)

Chapter Nineteen

7:45 PM –Outside CWP-TV

After finding the wrench in the box,
Otto left it but then changed the locks.
Gave it up carefully
To the RCUP
But was watched by a sly arctic fox.

The Colonel pulled up in a space opposite the studios and they sat, waiting for the Superintendent to arrive. No one had told the station manager that they were going to look in the CWP garage for the murder weapon. They'd leave that up to the Super to smooth over, if necessary.

Octavius said, "Let me do the talking first. I don't want Rowan to know of your brief encounter with Imperius Drake, Otto, or for that matter, your run-in with Pontius Puma, Condo."

"I never actually met the cat. I just destroyed his arms smuggling network. *(cf. Volume Two-The Case of the Spotted Band)* To this day, I don't think he knows what happened to his systems or who did it. I'd like to keep it that way."

"So would I," said the Bear, "That looks like the Superintendent walking up the street. OK, Showtime! Let's go."

Rowan was in plain clothes. He had exchanged his uniform horse blanket for a muted plaid number. The Wolf and Otter were wearing dark coats. Octavius had a muffler around his neck and otherwise trusted his heavy fur to keep him warm. The Condor had folded his wings over his body to keep out the cold.

"Let's get into this garage and out of the cold." said the Super. "I hope it isn't locked."

"It doesn't matter." Octavius replied as he walked over and pulled on the garage door handle. It didn't budge. "Are you up for a little breaking and entering, Superintendent? Otto, if you would, please."

The otter disappeared and in a few seconds the door lift whined into action. Otto was standing in the opening as the door reached its stops. The Superintendent whuffled, stared at Otto and said, "How…"

Octavius cut him off and said, "Let's get in out of the cold and we'll explain."

The four of them entered the dark garage. Otto lowered the door and turned on some shop lights.

"Our little friend here is pursuing a show business career as an illusionist. Only much of his act is not really illusion. As a participant in a series of experiments, his DNA and genetic structure have been altered and he has acquired a number of talents that have been very helpful to us in solving several major crimes. He can teleport. He can open and close locked doors, open padlocks, escape from bondage like the Great Whodunit. He also has

112

limited telekinesis. *(A dish antenna came flying toward them, stopped and returned to the table it was sitting on.)* Before you start having ideas about arresting him, I suggest you contact Superintendent Nigel Wardlaw of Shetland Yard and ask him how Otto helped us solve several murders, oil rig sabotage and attempted bombings. I'm afraid I can't be more specific than that except to ask Otto to give us one more demonstration. Otto please!"

The otter skittered over to a closet marked Computer Supplies. "Here's where I saw what I think is the murder weapon. A large wrench. Condo and I were scouting out the TV buildings to see if we could find anything the police may have missed. While I was here, an Arctic Fox came in, did some work on one of the computers and then opened the closet and put her laptop in it along with some papers. At the bottom of the closet is the wrench. She fastened the combination padlock on the door and left. I opened the padlock, *(Yes, I can do that.)* looked inside, put on a pair of work gloves and examined the wrench. There are stains on it that look like blood. I put it back, closed the closet, changed the combination and left. I'll open it for you now. No hocus pocus, I remembered the combination I put in."

He opened the door, pointed to the wrench and got out of the Superintendent's way. Caballus looked at the tool, picked up several papers in the closet, wrapped them around the wrench and took it out. "I'll give this to our lab right away. We need to concoct a story on how this was discovered and stick with it."

"How about we found it underneath one of the dumpsters. They didn't move them during the search, did they?" This from Condo. "We saw it and called you."

"Sounds a bit lame but it'll have to do. I suppose I should say, 'Thank you!'"

"Let's wait till we find out if it really is the weapon. You can also help by putting a muzzle around that Sergeant Preston. He's an officious twit."

The superintendent shrugged and nodded. "Oh wait, Senhor Condor. Didn't you have some thoughts aboot the TV station staff."

They walked outside, this time through one of the side doors leading into the alley which was still unlocked. The crime scene tape had been taken down.

"Well, si, I mean yes, almost the entire staff was in the studio when I did my interview with Senhorita Beatrice. There were only a very small number of animals who look big enough and powerful enough to have done her in. A couple of large wildcats, a bear, a ram, two caribou and that was it. Of course, there was also Wally Wapiti, the station manager but like the caribou and ram, he doesn't have claws."

"The perpetrator may have used something like claws although the medical examiner found traces of fur in one or two the wounds. He's not sure what kind of fur and he's sending to Ottawa for some analysis."

Otto piped up, "By the way, the two of us are coming back tomorrow to talk with Beatrice Beaver's administrative assistant. She walked the cow out of the building. You don't mind, do you?"

"If you hadn't found that wrench, I would tell you to mind your own damn business. But go ahead. See if you can garner any information from her that we didn't get. "I'll talk to you in the morning, Octavius, and we'll also see what Sergeant Preston has to say aboot the bar."

As they walked past the studio, they didn't notice the Arctic Fox staring after them. She was talking into her cell phone. "They found it. I don't know how. I locked it in the computer closet in the garage until I had a chance to take it and dump it in the river. Somebody tampered with the closet and changed the combination on the padlock. I couldn't get it open again. What did you say? Don't you call me that! Now look, I stuck my neck way out to help you and you better come through with your promises. You have a hell of a lot more to lose than I do. All right, I'll see you later at ten. Bring money!"

Frau Schuylkill

Chapter Twenty

8PM - Wednesday Ratison Hotel Lobby

What does all of her mystery mean?
Our Ms Bearyl decides to come clean.
Not a murderous heart!
She's just playing a part
From a famous Shakesbearean scene.

Frau Schuylkill was sitting in the lounge waiting for Bearyl to appear. She had checked the room the polars shared. Empty! Bearnice was over at Kitty's Kozy Korner with Lepi, Maury and Forrest trying to get that *dumbkopf* Sergeant to believe they were there on Monday. But no sign of Bearyl. This was getting irritating. Didn't she realize that her behavior was about to put her on the RCUP "person of interest" list if she wasn't there already. Stupid bear!

"Hi! Holding down the fort? You and I seem to be the only ones not out and "aboot" Winnipeg." The voice of Chita.

The Frau looked around and found herself staring at the diamond collar Chita always wore through rain, snow, sleet, dark of night, criminal and social occasions. "Good evening, Fraulein Catt. Or is it Frau? Are you still the mate of Pontius Puma?"

"A mistake soon to be rectified. I've applied for a Brazilian divorce. Infidelity and unusual cruelty. I'm going to try to get a huge settlement out of him. Not that I need the money. I just want to stick it to the bastard. I'm not sure he has any money left now that his empire has been destroyed and of course, he's sitting very uncomfortably in a U.S. jail. By the way, I am using Madame Catherine Catt as my nom de plume and identity any time police are involved. It's good for a little light entertainment. I could use a drink. How about you?"

"As long as we sit here in the lobby. I'm waiting to see if Bearyl makes an appearance."

"Where is she?"

"We don't know and that's a problem. I might as well tell you. Ever since the cow was killed Monday night, Bearyl has been acting very mysteriously."

"Oh, come on. You don't suspect her of having anything to do with a murder."

"It's not what I suspect. It's what the police might suspect. One of the bell-dogs saw her leave again right after she and Maury came back from trying to catch Bearnice and Lepi. That would be close to the time Honoria was killed. I don't think the police have heard the bell-dog's story but we have, and now she keeps disappearing and making up cover stories."

The cat scrunched up her nose and said, "That _is_ strange. I think better over a bowl of champagne. What's yours?"

"The same!"

Chita came back, walking erect and holding two large bowls of bubbly. She put one down next to the she-wolf. "There. Look! I'm sure you don't approve of me and frankly, my dear, I don't give a damn. However, the Colonel, Maury and I have reached rapprochement. The Bearoness and I are business partners in a genetics project. Otto has turned into my best pal. Lepi and I sang together in The Spotted Band. Bearyl and I arm wrestled those Scots oil rig owners into showing some common sense. I haven't had any serious face time with Howard or Bearnice but we seem to be OK. On the other hand, Octavius bearly tolerates me and would love to see me in prison. I strongly suspect you share the bear's feelings. I'm not suggesting we arrange a love fest *(the wolf snorted.)* but I do believe we could be of mutual benefit to each other. I'm smart. You're smart. I'm pretty good in a fight and so are you. I'm fast and you're fast."

"Faster" *(The Frau had mastered "Höchstgeschwindigkeit" hyperspeed.)*

"OK, faster, but between us we can catch any animal that tries to escape or elude us. Speaking of elusive, look who's coming through the revolving door. Ms Bearyl Blanc. Bearyl, come join us!!" she shouted

"Oh, hi Chita! Hello Frau Schuylkill. I was just on my way up to the room to see Bearnice and find out how they made out with the policeman."

"They haven't come back yet," said the Frau, "Do join us. Madame Catherine and I are having champagne. Would you like a bowl?"

119

"Well OK, but just one. I have a few things I have to do before going to bed. Since when are you Madame Catherine?"

Chita signaled the bartender for another bowl. "It's a handy pseudonym, especially when the police are around. Well, we haven't really spoken since our little adventure with the oil rig owners. I got a big kick out the way you got that jerk, Pringle, to drink that bowl of White Lightning. I thought he was going to die on the spot."

The Frau interrupted, "Speaking of dying, Ms Bearyl, there hasn't been any real progress in tracking down who killed the heifer. I hope the police will be satisfied that Mr. Leperello and your sister had nothing to do with it."

"Well, they certainly should. I know we both have tempers but Bearnice would never hurt a fly. Neither would Lepi."

"How about you?" asked the Frau.

"Whaaat!?"

"All right, let's get down to it. Monday night, you were seen by one of the bell-dogs going back out of the hotel after you had returned with Herr Maury. Just about enough time to get to the TV station and kill off the cow at ten o'clock. Since then, you've been evading all of us and the police. You lied about being down in the wardrobe department trying on Bearnice's dresses. No one there remembers seeing you and oh, yes, we cancelled that maple leaf costume the day before."

"Have you gone crazy, Frau Schuylkill. I can't believe you'd think…"

"I don't think but the police may, if that bell-dog tells his story to them and the wardrobe mistress tells about your lying."

"C'mon Bearyl," said Chita, "it's fess-up time. What the hell have you been doing since you got to Winnipeg and please don't give us that 'I've been catching up with old friends routine.'"

"Well, in fact, I have been catching up but not with old friends. The Manitoba Theatre Company is casting for its coming season and I'm auditioning for Lady Macbearth. I think I have the part. They keep calling me back. One more round and I'll know for sure."

The cat chirped, "That's great. Why all the secrecy?"

"Because I'll be letting down the team, especially the Bearoness. Bearnice has her concert series. We won't be able to fly the SST together. Frau, you and the Colonel have just started getting checked out on the Concorde and we were supposed to get up to speed on the Ursa Major. Probably not going to happen. We never anticipated that Belinda would be out of action for eight months or more and we don't have a full back-up crew. On top of that, I still have a part with the Aquabears. And I haven't told Maury any of this and he's supposed to be my agent. I feel awful."

"OK, maybe there's a wrinkle or two that needs to be ironed out but it sure as hell beats being arrested for murder. You're going to have to surface right away and keep the cops from getting wrong ideas. I assume you have plenty of witnesses from your tryouts."

"Oh God, Chita, too many. Every female animal in Canada seems to want the part. What do you think, Frau?"

"I agree with Madame Catt. Let's get the air cleared as soon as we can. You should probably start by talking with Herr Maury. After all, if you get the part, he has to be able to represent you. We need to talk with Herr Bear and of course, your sister. The rest can wait until we see whether you actually are chosen and how this investigation turns out. How long is the season?"

"Ten weeks with a possible road tour."

No sooner had she said that and the revolving door started twirling, unleashing a slightly tipsy Polar Bear and Himalayan Snow Leopard singing on the top of their substantial lungs:

"When I'm calling you-oo-oo oo-oo-oo!

"Will you answer too-oo-oo oo-oo-oo?"

And laughing hilariously. Right behind them came Forrest Fox, looking a bit less sober than usual and in the rear, as usual, good old me, Agent Maury, with a silly grin on my face.

The Frau turned to Bearyl and said, 'I don't think this is the time to make your little revelation. Tomorrow morning should be time enough."

Bearyl nodded.

Chita held out her paws to the merry minstrels and said, "I assume things went well?"

Lepi: "That, my amiga, is an understatement. Sergeant Preston has his sworn statement, signed by no fewer than fourteen Winnipeg citizens, tried and true, and notarized no less. Now we can get going full tilt on these concerts without looking over our shoulders every few minutes. Thanks to Forrest here and Maury. The whole event was a blowout. We had to sing at least five songs and have at least two or three drinks before Kitty and Maxie would let us go. Maury, can you please get them those front row tickets we promised them?"

I nodded, "With pleasure!"

Forrest cleared his throat. "I believe my services are no longer needed. I will settle accounts with Dr. Bear."

Bearnice hugged the fox. "Oh Forrest, thank you, thank you. Would you and your mate like to come to one of the recitals? We can get them tickets, too. Can't we, Maury?"

I nodded yes and Forrest, recovering from the exuberant hug said, "It would be our great pleasure, Bearnice. After hearing a sample this evening, I look forward to listening to the two of you in formal concert."

Hail, hail the gang's all here. Octavius, Colonel Where, Otto and Condo came in and joined the happy hooligans. We were creating quite a stir in the lobby.

"I assume from the gaiety, that things went well with Sergeant Preston," Octavius rumbled.

Bearnice hiccupped and giggled, "You mean Prissy Preston? That's what Kitty and Maxie call him. It fits! Oh, yes! It went shwimmingly, I mean swimmingly. We got over half of Winnipeg to swear they saw us at Kitty's Kozy Korner on Monday night. Prissy has a sworn and notarized statement to that effect in his hot little paws. Now maybe we can concentrate on what we're supposed to do – sing. Tra-la!" Another hiccup.

Octavius looked at Forrest and said, "Thank you Forrest! You've been a great help. Please send me your bill and I will see to it immediately. I don't think we need bother you any further unless you're curious about who really killed the cow. We don't know yet but we did turn over a bloodied wrench to the Superintendent. It might well be the murder weapon. It's up to the lab to determine."

Bearnice, who had turned into quite a chatterbox, giggled again and said, "Forrest and his mate are coming to one of recitals so we'll see him again."

Forrest smiled at Bearnice and turned to Octavius. "I would appreciate knowing the final outcome of the investigations. I suppose I could get that from Superintendent Caballus but I'd rather hear the full story from you, if and when you know it."

Octavius shrugged, "I'd like to hear the full story as well. This thing is beginning to irk me. Now, what about tomorrow morning?"

Otto said, "Condo and I are going back to the TV station to talk to Beatrice Beaver's administrative assistant. She walked the heifer out of the studios and with the exception of the killer, may have been the last one to see her alive. Before you ask, we have considered her as a possible accomplice. We'll find out tomorrow."

Octavius turned to the condor and asked, "Didn't you mention several animals working at the station who were big enough to have killed Honoria? I think you mentioned wildcats and a grizzly bear. Let's check them out further. I'm sure the Police interviewed them but at the time they were convinced that Lepi and Bearnice were the culprits so the interviews may have been a bit cursory, so to speak."

"We'll talk to them while we're there," said Condo.

"OK, let's the rest of us get together at ten tomorrow and brainstorm. Not you two. You go to your rehearsal. Colonel, could you go with them? I'm still not comfortable about leaving them unguarded while this killer is on the loose. He or she may have some sort of grudge on singers and voice coaches."

The Colonel nodded agreement but was nudged by the Frau. He walked off a little distance with her. "I think we've solved our Bearyl mystery," she whispered, "She wants to be Lady Macbearth."

"Huh?"

Chapter Twenty One

8AM Thursday - Ratison Hotel

Felicia the fox is found dead,
Strangle marks and a bruise on her head.
Same M. O. and same site
Did she put up a fight?
Or was she just bushwhacked instead?

The room phone rang. Several times! I pulled my head out from under the pillow, checked the time and looked blearily at the insistent instrument of torture. I hadn't asked for a wake-up call or room service so that left just one alternative – Octavius.

"Hullo!"

"Get dressed and get up here ASAP. Bring Otto, Condo, the Frau and the Colonel with you. Do not bring the Polars or Lepi. Do not bring Chita. There's been another murder!" (Click!) Octavius at his majestic best, growling orders and marshalling the troops.

Needless to say, it took me more than a few minutes to gather the desired cadre and proceed to Octavius' suite. He, of course, was in an impatient snit and I got the benefit of his annoyance. Been there, done that! But there are compensations which I kept in the front of mind as he began his tirade.

"I just got a call from Superintendent Caballus. Beatrice Beaver's assistant has been found dead in practically the same spot as the cow. Broken neck and claw marks. This time he wants us to bring in Bearyl for questioning. I told him that was patent nonsense but he was in no mood to be contradicted and I was in no mood to go at him until I understood what the hell was going on with her. Where has she been? What has she been doing? And why is Madame Catherine here? Now you have me calling her that. I specifically told you..."

"I'm here because Bearyl confessed to the Frau and me last night that she had been playing hooky auditioning for a part in The Manitoba Theatre Company's upcoming production of Macbearth. Excuse me, The Scottish Play. She thinks she may have the part of Lady Macbearth. She's been trying to keep it a secret. Right, Frau?"

"Ja, Herr Bear, Chita is correct. She was going to open up once she got the part. She is concerned everyone will think she is letting the team down leaving for ten weeks or more with the Theatre. She is torn and upset."

"Well, she's going to be more upset when she finds out the RCUP wants to talk to her. They think the Arctic Fox was killed at about ten o'clock. If it's the same murderer, he or she has a thing about that time and place."

Otto whistled, "Could that be the same Arctic Fox I saw with the bloody wrench in the garage? Was she Beatrice Beaver's assistant? She led the cow out of the station and maybe right into the alley where the murderer was waiting for her. Could this be a falling out among villains?"

Octavius frowned, "You may be right, Otto. Let's try that out on the Super. But first, where was Bearyl last night around ten."

"With me," said Chita, "we were talking show business into the wee small hours along with reminiscing about the Shetland Oil Rig caper."

Octavius frowned again, "Oh swell, a highly reliable witness with a trail of "wanted" citations as long as Lepi's tail. If you try to testify in front of the Superintendent, especially with your alias, you'll probably be hauled off to answer warrants in thirty or forty countries. Damn it, wasn't anybody else there?"

"We all broke up about 9:30 or so." I said. "Hey, wait a minute! What about the bartender or the bell-dog. They'd remember if the two of you were sitting and ordering drinks."

The Colonel snorted, "Here we go again with the bartender. He might have thought Bearyl was Bearnice."

The Frau interrupted, "The bell-dog won't. He knows about the ankle bracelet Bearnice wears. If he was on duty last night, we can get him to testify that it was Bearyl with Chita."

"All right. The Superintendent is waiting for us at CWP. Frau Schuylkill, please get Bearyl. Colonel, I'm sorry but I'd still like you to stay with the singers. Even more so after this crime. Maury, Otto and Condo! Come with us. I want as many brains working on this one as we can spare. Maury, call Forrest Fox. We may need him for round two. Coming Chita or are you Madame Catherine at the moment?"

128

"Oh, what the hell," said the Cat, "I wasn't doing anything important anyway."

Needless to say, Bearyl wasn't overjoyed at the way things were going. She was more concerned about missing her last audition this afternoon than she was about being suspected by the police.

We piled into the ATV and a couple of cabs and proceeded to the CWP alley. Crime scene tape was in profusion. Several police cars were parked near the entrance. I looked around. One positive note, Sergeant Preston wasn't among them. The Super was. So was Wally Wapiti and Beatrice Beaver who was sobbing her eyes out. The Medical Examiner was making final notes before removing the body.

Caballus whinnied and strode over. "I see you've brought your gang, Octavius. We have the investigation in hand, thank you. This is Bearyl Blanc? Sorry, I can't tell you apart from your sister."

"Bearnice wears an ankle bracelet and I don't. Why am I a suspect?"

"You're merely a person of interest at this point along with quite a few others. Felicia Foxx was clawed and then strangled and we are checking any animals associated with the prior case who seem capable of doing her in. You certainly meet those criteria."

Condo came on with a voice reminiscent of Humphrey Bogart and said, "There are several wildcats and a grizzly bear on the staff here. I assume you're looking at them, too. Even a ram and a wapiti."

"We are, Mr. Condor, we are."

Otto had disappeared behind the crime scene tape and was looking over the Medical Examiner's shoulder. He skittered back and looked at the horse. "That's her, Superintendent. That's the fox I told you about when we found the wrench. She was the one hiding it in the computer supply closet."

"Are you sure of that?"

"Absolutely. First Arctic Fox I ever saw who wears diamond bangle earrings and a matching bracelet. The face is the same, too."

"Well, that helps to further confirm our suspicions that the two crimes are tied together. She's too small to be the cow's killer but she may have been his or her accomplice."

Condo leaned over. "We were coming over this morning to interview her. Beatrice Beaver says she was the one who walked Honoria Heifer out of the TV station after the show. She might have walked her right into her death."

Octavius harrumphed, *(shades of Sergeant Preston)* "Anyway, we can confirm the fact that Bearyl Blanc was in the company of Madame Catherine Catt at the Ratison Hotel last night at the assumed time of this murder. Madame Catt is the Editor-in-chief and Publisher of two highly popular female magazines, *PURR* and *SOW*, based in London. She is here to cover the recitals, having written and run two earlier issues on Bearnice and Mr. Leperello. When she discovered that Ms Bearyl Blanc is an actress, currently in try-outs for The Manitoba Theatre Company's next Shakesbearean production, she felt there might be a related story – two show business twins –

and she decided to interview Bearyl. Several members of the Ratison staff will bear out their presence in the lobby lounge at ten and later. Isn't that correct, Madame Catt, Ms Blanc?"

Chita almost choked but blurted out a strong affirmative and Bearyl said, "That's exactly what we were doing."

"Well, Rowan" said Octavius, "if you think we can't be of any further assistance here, we do have other tasks to perform. We'll keep you informed on anything we find out and hope you will do the same. Shall we go, folks?"

Chita waited until Octavius had struggled into the ATV and said, "That was the smoothest piece of "fact interpretation" I have ever heard. Thank you for not revealing my true identity. Apparently, the Super is not up on his International Wanted Posters."

"I did it for Bearyl. She needed a credible witness so I made you credible. However, I still believe you are one of the most incredible criminals I have ever encountered. By the way, does your sister Cyd really exist or is she another one of your aliases?"

"The cat winked and said, "I'll never tell!"

Just then Forrest Fox arrived.

Octavius waved at him and said, "Too late, Forrest, the police have cleared Bearyl. Sorry to have brought you out."

"That's OK," replied the lawyer. "Maybe I'll stick around for few minutes. Never know who might need an attorney."

Neither do I. I told Octavius to leave with Bearyl, Madame Catherine and the Frau. Otto, Condo and I were going to stay on and go ahead with a few more interviews. Of course, our first target was on her way to the morgue but there were some other folks to talk to. All this, of course, if we were allowed to do so by the RCUP.

Chapter Twenty Two

10 AM Thursday – On the way back to the Hotel

Grigor Gregory sang, don't you see.
Now he works at CWP.
He once trained with the cow
But he hates her, and how
Something really seems fishy to me.

Octavius was seated in the flat bed of the ATV with Bearyl. Frau Schuylkill was driving and Chita was sitting in the shot gun seat up front. She was also trying to pick up on the conversation she and the Frau were having last night that had been interrupted by Bearyl's arrival.

"Frau Schuylkill, may I call you Ilse?"

"That is my name."

"Well, Ilse, as I was saying last night, we have a lot of similar talents that might come in handy in certain situations."

"Perhaps, but of course, you will be returning to your publications in London and we will be commuting between Cincinnati and the Shetlands. I don't see us having too many opportunities to work together, and of course, The Colonel and I are partners in many of Herr Bear's activities." *(And in many of their own activities. Ah lupine romance!)*

"Oh, I realize that, but sometimes a little female intuition and cunning can go a long way in managing events. For example, what's your take on this latest murder? I wonder if Miss Felicia pushed the cow's murderer a bit too far. I'm convinced she was in on Honoria's demise. 'Come with me, Madame Heifer. Let me call you a cab. While we're waiting why don't we step into this alleyway and get out of the cold. Slash and crash. Oh dear, maybe we don't need that cab after all.' And then, according to Otto, she was assigned the task of disposing of the murder weapon. A task she didn't carry out quite as planned. That may have done for her or maybe she was trying a little blackmail. Whoever the cow's killer is, he or she has quite a fierce temper. No weapon this time. Strangulation of a much smaller victim with a few claw slashes thrown in. Do you agree?"

"It sounds logical. It also makes it more likely that the killer is a member of the TV station staff. I wonder how Herr Maury, Otto and the Condor are progressing, if at all?"

*****

Well, here we are still at CWP-TV. Condo, Otto and your obedient servant, Mauritius Meerkat. The police are not being very forthcoming or liberal with their agreement to let us make inquiries. We did learn that it was one of the remote crews who found Felicia. We spoke for a moment with Beatrice Beaver but between her sobbing and lisping, we didn't get much that was helpful.

We ran into the grizzly bear who had been in the studio during Condo's interview with Beatrice. I guess the constabulary hadn't gotten to him yet in their inquiries. He asked Condo for another demonstration of the voice unit and pelted him with questions aboot the technology involved, most of which went right over Otto's and my head. We did discover that he was going to be the producer-director of the recordings of Lepi's and Bearnice's Saturday and Sunday recitals. Seems he has a background in classical music. Something clicked. I remember the Music Director at the Opera mentioning one of Honoria's students was a grizzly named…What? What? What? Gregory or Gregor or Grigor. He was dumped by the Opera for fighting or something like that.

"I'm sorry! We've never really been introduced. My name is Mauritius Meerkat and this gentlebeast is simply called Otto."

The Condor was all apologies for not having done the formalities. The grizzly shook our paws and said, "My name is Grigor Gregory."

"Mr. Gregory, I'm sorry to have to ask you this but weren't you a member of the Winnipeg Opera chorus?"

"Yes, I was. How did you know that?"

"We asked the Music Director for a list of names of Honoria Heifer's students. We're helping the RCUP in their investigation of her murder. Your name was on that list."

"Yeah, well, that was one of the bigger mistakes of my short singing career. I signed on with her for two months. She was worse than useless and cost too damn much. I dropped her but she wouldn't give me any of my money back. The bitch! Sorry, but I get angry just thinking about it. I also believe she got me fired from the Opera Company but I can't prove it. That was OK. This job pays a lot better and I wasn't headed for stardom anyway."

Condo looked him in the eye. He was tall enough. "You do realize that what you just told us makes you a prime suspect in Honoria's murder."

"What the hell? Are you crazy? I didn't go near that cow, even when she was in the studio for her interview. Everything I told you happened a couple of years ago. If I had wanted to kill her off, I would have done it then."

I said, "We're obligated to tell the police everything we learn or we'll be in trouble for withholding evidence. You could probably use a good lawyer. We just happen to know one who has been specializing in bears, recently. He happens to be here at the station right now. His name is Forrest Fox. Don't worry. I'll get my boss, Octavius Bear, to pick up his fee, if you're not guilty. If you are, then it's your problem. Do you want me to call Forrest?"

"I guess so," he growled. "I should never have talked to you guys. Yeah, call him. I don't know any lawyers."

I got Forrest just as he was about to leave. He was in the lobby. I explained the situation and asked him to join us in Studio B.

"Well," he said as he came in the door. "My cup runneth over. Bears, bears, and more bears! You don't happen to have a wildcat or two stashed away somewhere, do you? Hello, I'm Forrest Fox, partner in Fox, Fox and Fox specializing in criminal cases and this thing with Honoria Heifer is certainly a criminal case."

The grizzly shambled over and shook paws. "Hello, Mr. Fox."

"Call me Forrest!!"

"OK, I'm Grigor Gregory. Grigor is fine."

"Right, well, following a similar trail of activity with other former suspects in the heifer's death, the first thing we need to establish is that you couldn't have been on the spot when the crime, excuse me, crimes were committed."

"Crimes??"

"Yes, the Police are convinced the death of Honoria Heifer and Felicia Foxx are connected."

"Felicia's dead?'

"Yes, Clawed and strangled last night in just about the same spot as the cow."

"I didn't know. I was cooped up here in the studio planning out the coverage of the recitals and I guess I fell asleep. I only woke up a couple of hours ago."

"Was anyone with you?"

"My production assistant, Charlie, was here for a while. He was still here when I fell off, I think."

"Any idea where he might be right now?"

"Probably at home or on his way here. He's not due in until noon."

"I think the Police are going to want to talk to both of you," said Condo.

"I guess you're right but the timing sure stinks. I've got to get the taping of the recitals off the ground right now."

"I'm sorry, Grigor. But we have to pass this on to the RCUP right away. What do you think, Forrest?"

"Give me a little time to speak with my client-to-be and then we can all go and speak to the Superintendent."

"OK, how much time do you need?

"Probably an hour. Maybe less if Charlie shows up soon."

"You've got it, unless, of course, the police show up on their own, beforehand."

"We'll deal with that, if we have to," said the Fox.

"Meanwhile, I want to do some more checking on Felicia Foxx. What, if any, is the tie-in between her and Honoria and for that matter, her and Honoria's killer. I wonder if Beatrice Beaver has recovered from her hysterics yet? I think we also want to talk to the Station Manager."

The otter replied, "Let's give it shot, Maury. How about you, Condo?"

"I'm in. *(His micro-electronic voice prosthetic was set on Mid-Western American with a touch of Las Vegas gambler tossed in.)* Let's meet in an hour, Forrest. We'll come to you since you have to wait for Charlie to make his appearance."

Chapter Twenty Three

10 AM Thursday –Main Stage at the Opera

Beatrice Beaver tells Otto and me
That Ms Foxx was behaving quite free.
Got Honoria set
For an interview, yet
She got nobody else to agree.

A few overhead flood lights were all the illumination available on the concert hall stage. Hartley, the Orchestra Leader; Giselle, the accompanist; and the Musical Director, Herr Professor Doktor Dieter von Tripp made their way up the main aisle with Bearnice, Lepi and the Colonel in tow. Hartley made his way backstage and in a few seconds, the stage was aglow. A few lights in the house also came on giving the singers a taste of what a sold out audience might look like. *(if you had a pretty good imagination.)* The balcony remained dark.

The Musical Director looked at them. "Well. Here it is. Not the Edinbeargh Opera House but a good venue, nonetheless. I'll put the acoustics in this place up against any other similarly sized concert hall in the world. Here's today's plan. Hartley and Giselle will take you though the program with a piano this morning. Then we'll do a second run so the TV people can get their blocking set up. They'll fill in the details on that tomorrow morning when we have the full orchestra on hand. And of course, that's when we'll do the full dress rehearsals with lighting cues and all the rest, eh."

"By the way, this morning is the last chance we have to decide to run a second performance on Sunday. Can you get your agent on the phone and discuss it with him right now? If you do want to go ahead with a performance on Sunday evening, we have to alert the press; talk to the musician's union and other support groups; set up ticket sales, take out advertising and lots of other things."

Lepi turned to Bearnice. "Are you up for doing another or not?"

"I'd like to. How about you?"

"Hey, I certainly could use the extra money and the additional exposure. I think we're in good enough shape provided we stay out of Kitty's Kozy Korner. Do you have any thoughts on it, Colonel?"

"No, my current job is keeping you guys safe. If you don't think you'll wear yourselves out, go for it. You might also want to talk to Madame Catherine and Octavius."

"Let's call Maury first."

They did and they got me on the first ring. We backed and filled a bit but finally decided to give it a go. Octavius originally wanted to leave Winnipeg the minute the Sunday matinee was over but now with this Honoria Heifer-Felicia Foxx mess in full swing plus the question of what to do if Bearyl got the part of Lady Macbearth, his schedule had to become more flexible. He wouldn't be happy about it but once on a case, he got very tenacious.

*****

Speaking of whom, we last left our oversized hero sitting in the flat bed of the ATV with Bearyl, discussing the ins and outs of appearing in the Scottish play for at least ten weeks; getting backup crews for the SST; transporting Lepi and Bearnice to their next concert. *(Toronto in 3 weeks)* Bearyl's role in the Aquabears review was a non-problem. The show, *Some Like it Cold*, was on hold pending Bearoness Belinda's giving birth and recuperating. As for the Concorde, Belinda had employed several SST crews before the polar twins. Octavius would have the Frau do a search to see if any of them would be available, especially at the rates that the Bearoness and Octavius would be willing to pay.

They pulled up in front of the hotel. Octavius trundled out. Chita went off in search of her photographer who was due to arrive shortly and the Frau and Bearyl drove off again, this time for the theater and the try-outs. The Frau decided to stay with Bearyl as protection.

As Octavius shambled toward the elevator and his room, he got a call from me back at CWP-TV.

"Hello," I said, "Things are moving along apace over here but I can't say we're making any progress. We may be going backwards."

"Explain!"

"We have another suspect. He's a producer-director at CWP and will be handling the taping of the recitals, provided he doesn't get arrested first. A grizzly bear called Grigor Gregory who briefly studied with Madame Heifer

142

several years ago. He gave up on her, tried to get his money back, failed and has been carrying a grudge ever since. He may or may not have an alibi for Felicia Foxx's murder. Anyway, I made a few executive decisions. We passed the information on to the RCUP. I called in Forrest Fox to support Grigor and told him you'd pay for it if the bear was not guilty."

"Playing a bit fast and loose with my money, aren't you? What's your personal take on this guy?"

"I don't think he did either of the dirty deeds but the police can certainly build a case if they want to. If he is the killer, he's pretty forthcoming about his feelings against the cow and he swore he didn't know the admin assistant was dead until we told him."

Octavius came up with one of his world-famous "Hmmms."

"OK. Let's leave that in Forrest's paws for the moment. See what more you can dig up about Felicia but don't get in the RCUP's way. I'm going to call the Colonel and see how the rehearsal is going."

"Oh, that's another thing. We're going to have a third recital on Sunday night. The Opera is really eager to run another session. Lepi and Bearnice say they are up for it and they could use the money and the extra exposure. I agreed. I know that screws up your original travel plans but I thought you wanted to hang on here until something like a solution to the murders rears its head."

"Well, Theatrical Agent Maury on the loose. Just don't let them burn themselves out. For all their talent, they are still fundamentally amateurs. What are Condo and Otter up to?"

"Roaming the halls, studios and offices here at CWP until either management or the police throws us all out. We're especially looking for leads and whatever ties Felicia Foxx may have had with the killer. I'll bet next month's salary (!) that she aided and abetted and then pushed it too far. Especially after Otto and Condo spotted her with the wrench. Did they analyze that yet? Was it the murder weapon?"

"I haven't heard from the Super yet. They also found some traces of fur in several of the cow's wounds. They sent them to Ottawa for closer analysis."

"So we are firmly in mid-air. Any news from the Shetlands?"

"No news is good news. Bel seems to be sleeping her way peacefully through gestation but you just gave me an idea if the RCUP hasn't thought of it first. I suggested that Superintendent Caballus call Superintendent Wardlaw at Shetland Yard to check out Otto's many unique talents and how he helped in the Scottish case. I don't know if he ever did. I'm going to contact Wardlaw myself and see if he can give us any more information on the late, unlamented Madame Honoria. I think she operated from the Edinbeargh Opera, or at least that's where Belinda found her when she was looking for a coach for Lepi and Bearnice. Not like the Bearoness to make a mistake like that. Maybe she came highly recommended by someone who was in the cow's debt or worse."

"Well," I said, "given the number of students she seemed to keep losing, I wonder how she made a living. A pretty good living from all appearances. Maybe she had few sidelines."

"That's what I want Shetland Yard to look into. Let me know what you find out about Felicia."

I closed the connection and went off to join Condo and Otto who, in turn were in search of Beatrice Beaver and/or Wally Wapiti. As I skittered along the office bay, I noticed one of Condo's wings draped over a cubicle wall. It looks like they found Beatrice. An RCUP constable was just finishing up taking her statement while Otto and Condo stood by. The cop seemed to be only interested in Beatrice's whereabouts *(Sorry! whereaboots)* last night. She told him she had finished her show at 9, packed up her stuff and headed home. She left some notes for Felicia for the morning but she hadn't actually seen her again after the show began. This seemed to satisfy the policeman. He nodded to us and walked off.

I stuck my nose in the cubicle. Otto was sitting in a corner chair. Condo was half in and half out with his wingspan making things tight. I slipped in under Condo's wing.

"Hi, Ms Beaver. Feeling better? You seemed terribly upset about Ms Foxx's death. Were you two close?"

"Close?? Ha! I couldn't stand the bitch. Neither could anyone else around here. She was an ambitious little trouble-maker. I've been trying for months to get Wally to ditch her but he wouldn't hear of it."

145

Condo cut in, "Sorry, Ms Beaver, but I couldn't help noticing you've lost your lisp."

"Oh that! That's a bit of show biz shtick Morley Moose and I tossed in when I first started here. It began as a joke but the viewers loved it so, I left it in. I tweak him aboot his big nose and he comes back aboot my big teeth. It's getting a bit tired but as long as it helps the ratings the lisp stays. Oh, and call me Beatrice."

"If you weren't that close with Ms Foxx, why the hysterics?"

"Because I may be next. It looks like anyone who had anything to do with that stuck up cow is in danger."

"I really doubt that, but it would be wise if you stayed out of dark alleys until we catch this guy."

"You think it's a guy?"

"Both of these killings required some extra physical strength. The police only recently ruled out Bearnice and Bearyl Blanc but they believed the Polar Bears were strong enough and of course, had formidable claws. Fortunately, we were able to prove that neither was anywhere near the scene at the time of the killings. But after you eliminate those two, the culprit is probably a male. Probably someone Felicia knew."

She blinked, "Do you think she had anything to do with killing the cow?"

Otto nodded. "We've uncovered some evidence linking her to the weapon. The police have put a lid on any more information and please do not use that on your program. That could put you in danger."

She blinked again. "You know, there was something funny aboot this whole thing from the start. Whenever there is any entertainment news coming up, I want to be there to chat with the principals, usually the stars or the director or the author. Animals like that. I don't think we ever had a voice coach on, for God's sake. I wanted the two singers and I hope we have them for tomorrow night's show. I don't know whether Felicia arranged that or not."

"I'm their agent and she didn't arrange anything with me but I'm sure we can handle that before I leave. I know Bearnice and Lepi would love to have a chance to speak for themselves after the fiasco Honoria made of her interview. One prohibition though. No mention of the Heifer's murder. No questions about her at all. Agreed?"

"Sure. Now what were we talking aboot? Oh, yes! Felicia set up this appearance of the cow without asking anyone, including me. Not the way we usually do things. She was very insistent aboot it. It was going to be a light news night so I didn't push back very much. The other odd thing was I didn't get to chat with the Heifer before her appearance. Felicia said she would brief her and she'd be fine. Well, she didn't turn out to be fine. What a smug, self important pain in the ass she turned out be. I was delighted when Felicia escorted her out of the studio. I felt like hitting her myself."

"Beatrice," I choked, "Watch what you say. We already have enough suspects without putting you on the list."

"Oh, who's on the list?"

"Nice try, lady. You news folks can't pass up a possible scoop, can you? Once again, if you bring up Honoria's death with Lepi or Bearnice, I will do my best to get you and your lisp fired the hell out of here. A promise is a promise. One last question, from me at least."

I looked quizzically at Condo and Otto. Shrugs! No takers!

"Was there anyone outside the station that Felicia might have had dealings with?"

"I don't know. I tried to stay as far away from her personal life as possible."

"How about at the Opera? The request to put Honoria on may have come from there. You didn't ask for her. I doubt whether Felicia would even know who she was."

"You may be right, Mr. Meerkat. It may have happened that way but I wouldn't know who to tag with it. Probably the Communications or Public Relations folks at the Opera. After all, we are going to tape and broadcast the recitals."

"True, well I'll be heading over there shortly. I'll ask around. Thanks for your help. And Beatrice..."

"Yes??"

"Keep the lishp!!"

Chapter Twenty Four

11:30 AM Thursday – The Main Stage at the Opera

At the Opera, searching for clues
With a roster of staff interviews.
Sorting out who is who.
What is false? What is true?
Looking out for some usable news.

Bearnice and Lepi had just finished their fourth number when I arrived in the auditorium. I had stopped off at the office of Godfrey, the Associate Director, to arrange for center row tickets to be held at the box office for Kitty and Maxie as well as Forrest and his mate. I also made sure that all the members of Octavius' team were going to have good seats at each performance. Madame Catherine Catt would get special treatment. Good print and on-line publicity for The Opera.

The Great Bear turned out to be a bit of a problem. The Century Concert Hall did not have seats sizeable enough to accommodate his bulk, even in the Large Animals section. Money to the rescue! The house crew was put into action depopulating the chairs in one of the boxes and replacing them with a single, purpose-built rig. As I scanned around the hall, checking the best seats with Godfrey, I looked up to the darkened balcony. I thought I made out a shadowy figure with glowing eyes. As Octavius would say, "Hmm!" Oh well, could have been anyone getting a free preview.

The Music Director, Stage Manager and Orchestra Leader were taking turns giving instructions to the singers, setting up light cues and checking the acoustics. Such things run slowly. Later this afternoon, the TV people would be on site and the process would begin again. Time for some more data gathering. I asked Godfrey who on the staff would have arranged Honoria's appearance on Beatrice Beaver's show Monday night.

"Either our Communications Manager or Public Relations Manager would have handled it. I can arrange for you to meet them, if you like. Is there some kind of problem?"

"I don't know. We're just trying to trace the whole process leading up to her death. I think I told you that in addition to being a theatrical agent, I'm also a detective working with Octavius Bear who among many things is a world famous sleuth. When our singers were first accused by the police of killing the cow, we swung into action to help prove them innocent. Now that we're immersed in it, Octavius and his crime team, six of us in all, are working with the RCUP to solve the killings."

"Killings? Are there more than one?"

"Yes, this morning Felicia Foxx, an administrative assistant at CWP-TV was found dead in practically the same place and in very similar circumstances."

"Felicia Foxx," said Godfrey, "Now that's a name I recognize. She worked here for a while in the Director's office but left about a year ago to join CWP. I guess classical music wasn't glamorous enough for her."

"I'd appreciate meeting your Communications and PR managers. But first, would you mind if I made a quick phone call? Only take a second!"

I walked a few steps away and dialed Condo. He answered with his Latin Lover voice.

"OK, Romeo, knock it off. It's me, Maury. Look, if you haven't thought of it already, you might want to check in with the station's security officer and find out what the story is on the non-functioning security cameras. The police may have covered it already but I'd like your techie opinion as to whether anything smells bad there."

"Gotcha Mo! *(Brooklynese)* He's on our visitation list. Anything new there?"

"Yeah, it seems Felicia Foxx worked at the Opera before going to CWP. In the Director's office."

"Isn't that interesting. The lady got around."

"I have to go. Talk to you later."

I returned to Godfrey and apologized. Off we went to Public Relations land.

The PR Manager was in fact a Manageress, a Masked Shrew named Cecily, Cecily Shrew. Godfrey did the introductions, told her why I was there and asked her to take me to the Communications Manager when we were through. He shook my paw with his wing and waddled away.

"Thanks for seeing me, Ms Shrew. As Godfrey explained, in addition to being the agent and business manager for Ms Blanc and Mr. Leperello, I am also part of a private investigative team that is working with the police on the murders of Honoria Heifer and Felicia Foxx."

"Felicia Foxx, she's dead?"

"They found her body outside CWP this morning. It looks like she was killed in very similar circumstances to Madam Heifer."

"Oh well, small loss!"

"You knew her?"

"Everybody here knew her. She was an assistant in the Director's office and acted as if she was the Director. Tried to boss everyone around. Not a great way to make yourself popular. Big sigh of relief when she took off for CWP. I understand she wasn't beloved over there either. Anyway, how can I help you?"

"I'm trying to track how Madame Honoria got on the Beatrice Beaver show on Monday night. According to Beatrice, Felicia Foxx arranged it. Unfortunately, we can't interview her. But what I'm trying to understand is why Honoria would be interviewed anyhow. Especially when there are interviews of the two principals planned for tomorrow night."

"Sure, we set those up. But I had nothing to do with the voice coach's appearance. I wouldn't have approved it. I watched a replay of it. It was terrible. What a fake! Let's check with Marty. He's our Communications

Manager. TV activities come across both of our desks. He's managing our side of the CWP taping of the recitals this weekend. I handle the publicity angles, including interviews. A little messy but it works."

Marty turned out to be a Stone Marten who had immigrated to Canada from France. He turned up in Winnipeg after living in Quebec for a short time. I tried my Isle of Mauritius French on him and we ended up laughing uproariously at the result. Long story short, he had nothing to do with Honoria's interview but offered the intriguing idea that it was set up without the knowledge or instigation of anyone at the Opera meaning Felicia Foxx may have been working on her own. While I was at it, I asked him about Grigor Gregory, the producer-director of the upcoming recital tapings. That is, if the police didn't arrest him first. *(I didn't mention that item.)*

"Grigor? Great guy! Knowledgeable, cooperative, honest and knows his way around music. He was with our chorus for a while but I think he's happier in television. We've had some really first class productions working with him. Why do you ask?"

"In my role as agent for the two singers, I'm always concerned about anyone who is going to influence their image."

"They are in good paws with Grigor. He'll get them at their best and make it even better."

"Nice to know, Thanks for your help." *(Another damn good reason to make sure Forrest keeps Grigor out of the paws and hooves of RCUP.)* I called the lawyer.

"Hi, It's Maury Meerkat. Just checking in. If you want character witnesses for Grigor, I can get you a busload from the Opera and there are plenty at the TV station, too."

"I know. He seems to be a really sweet guy. The police haven't moved on it yet. I think they're waiting for the analysis of the bloodstains on the weapon. It seems there were two different stains. One was definitely the cow's but the other is different and unidentified. Then there are the hairs that were in the cow's wounds. Those were sent to Ottawa and nothing's come back yet."

"It's really important to the singers' careers that he is available to produce and direct the tapings. Here at the Opera, they seem to think he's an audio-visual miracle worker."

"Message received. I'm thinking of putting "Bears Our Specialty" on my business cards. I'll keep in touch."

Chapter Twenty Five

Noon Thursday -The Manitoba Shakesbearean Theatre

Here's a problem to ponder about!
The security system was out.
At CWP
There was nothing to see
When Honoria died from her clout.

Frau Schuylkill had explained to the show director and producer that until the killer or killers of Madame Honoria Heifer were caught, the police suggested maintaining a protective guard for the two singers. Since Bearyl was Bearnice's identical twin, they felt it would be wise to protect her as well. She further explained that she was a trained *(and armed)* security professional. She also promised she would be in no way interfering with the proceedings provided Bearyl was always in plain sight. She also felt reasonably certain that all this would be over very soon. She knew Bearyl was a true professional and the events of the last few days were not affecting her acting abilities one bit. Finally, she smiled showing her three or four thousand teeth.

It probably was the smile that did it but the show management invited her in and asked her to make herself comfortable.

"Now," said the director, "we have winnowed the candidates to play Lady Macbearth down to three and this afternoon's session will produce a principal and an understudy. Ladies, please take up your scripts and turn to Act I, Scene VII. I shall play Macbearth. Ms Black, let's begin with you."

And so it went into the early afternoon. Bearyl read second and then took a seat next to the Frau, waiting.

Finally, after three episodes of "screwing courage to the sticking-place," the tryouts ended. The producer, director and several other unidentified members of the company walked to the back of the rehearsal room. Head shaking, murmurs, checking notes. Signs of Agreement!

"Bearyl Blanc, please! Ms Blanc, you will be our Lady Macbearth. Ms Frost, you will be her understudy. Thank you, ladies. Rehearsals begin next Tuesday at 9 AM."

Bearyl went through a combination of giggles, snorts and sobs. She grabbed the Frau in a bear hug and spun her around. The she-wolf turned red with embarrassment. Then Bearyl took out her phone and called me. Needless to say, I was delighted. Then she gasped. "Oh, no! How are we going to get the Concorde back to Abeardeen? Bearnice can't leave before Monday and I have to be here Tuesday."

"We'll think of something," I said while thinking of absolutely nothing. Being an agent has its moments. Oh, boy!

*****

Phone messages to all and sundry on the team announcing Bearyl's triumph. The Colonel relayed the message to Bearnice and Lepi when they had a break in their rehearsal. Bearnice got on the phone immediately to her sister and they had a major giggle fest. The Frau was bringing Bearyl over to the Century Center to join them.

I called Octavius at the hotel. He was delighted. I didn't mention the logistics problem with the Concorde caused by her rehearsal demands. He had just finished up a conversation with Superintendent Wardlaw in the Shetlands. It seems Honoria had several sources of income in addition to her voice coach activities back in Scotland. A search of her bank records turned up sporadic deposits of sizeable amounts, usually in cash. She did not seem to have an accountant and the Police were still searching for her attorney, if she had one. The cow's popularity at the Edinbeargh Opera was not very high. Several members of the establishment wanted to send a congratulatory award to whoever had bumped her off. Ah, the dour Scots! The search continued to trace her income. Something didn't smell right.

Chita, who had caught up with her photographer, immediately went into stop the presses mode. This double sweep by the polar twins had to be a major feature in *SOW* Magazine's next edition. Big photo spread; joint interviews; play up the Bearoness' involvement; feature the SST. Never mind that it was a Winnipeg theatre group. They have won awards and will probably go on tour.

I called Forrest Fox and told him my news and he told me his. Charlie had finally showed up and corroborated Grigor's story aboot sleeping in the studio. He was conked out when Charlie left at midnight. Forrest was delighted that Bearyl was no longer under any suspicion. "Although," he chuckled, "if she had been involved, considering the character of Lady

Macbearth, there might have been an opportunity for a little type-casting." No thanks!

It occurred to me to call Beatrice Beaver. She picked right up on the idea and altered the Friday night interviews to include Bearyl. I had to make sure that Lepi didn't get pushed into the background. I couldn't imagine Chita shortchanging her old singing buddy in *PURR* Magazine but I had to have a further word with Beatrice.

When I reached Condo and Otto, they were about to join CWP's Security Officer to discuss the non-functioning security cameras. By the magic of omniscient narration, let's join them now.

*****

"When the security company and I finally agreed that it was time to begin the upgrade of the camera system, I sent out a memo to all department heads warning them that the rig would be down for several days. In retrospect, that might not have been a good idea. I just wanted them to be on a higher alert against strangers and to make sure all access points were kept tightly locked. In a TV complex, that's not easy. We always have folks roaming in and out as part of the programming or production work." This from Cody Coyote, former member of the RCUP, current Security Officer at CWP-TV.

"What did the upgrades consist of?" asked Condo.

"Wider angle, sharper focus, colour cameras. Sensor driven automatic tracking. Increased sensitivity on the microphones. Four additional camera installations to eliminate the blind spots. Upgraded recording systems with back up storage. Several more interior monitors for the security staff. Computer search and comparison apps. Training for all the staff. Immediate relay to the local Police. In short, we are moving into the twenty-first century. It took a helluva lot of persuasion but a plague of area break-ins last year finally convinced the Board of Directors."

"So," said Otto, "it was pretty common knowledge that the system would be down, at least for conversion and cutover purposes."

"Unfortunately, it turned out to be longer than we thought. Vendor issues, wrong equipment, failed tests. Even with our contingency plan, we were off-line more than I should have tolerated. Part of the system is still down. The alley, for one thing. Damned ironic. That's where the murders took place."

"Who's the vendor or vendors?"

"That's the other problem. The Finance Office insisted we go for low bidder and we ended up with a shop I had never heard of before. Manitoba Detection. Someone on our staff had a relative that worked for them, probably fed them information on the bids and they low-balled the price. Yeah, I know. It smells."

"Do you know who that staff member is?"

"Was! It was Felicia Foxx. Ain't that a kick?"

Otto looked at Condo. "Maybe we should talk with Manitoba Detection after we check in with Octavius and the RCUP Superintendent."

Chapter Twenty Six

3 PM Thursday - The Ratison Hotel

With our talks almost out of the way,
Just one more and we call it a day.
Talk with him and we're done.
The Director's the one.
Seems Felicia was once his PA.

After my round of interviews at the Opera and a quick late lunch, I ended up in Octavius' suite at the hotel. Condo and Otto were on their way to join us. The Colonel was still playing guard for the singers and the Frau was with Bearyl.

"While we wait for Otto and Senhor Condor, I'm going to do a last minute check with the Colonel and the Frau," he said. "I want to make sure we have our stories all straight before we get together with Superintendent Caballus. We're meeting with him at five here in the hotel. The wolves should be available then. Do you think I should invite Forrest Fox?"

"Oh yes!" I replied, "If for no other reason than to get Grigor off the hook. I think the two of them are over at the Opera, plotting out the TV moves while Lepi and Bearnice rehearse yet again. Tomorrow's a full dress rehearsal with the orchestra and the full TV Crew. Then Saturday and show time. We are going through with the second recital on Sunday evening. By the way, we have something of a logistics issue on our hands. Getting the SST back to

Abeardeen. Bearnice will be available Monday and so will Bearyl **_BUT_** Bearyl has to be back here Tuesday morning for her first rehearsal. Not enough time for her to come back on a commercial flight."

"OK, Octavius Bear, Patron of the Arts to the rescue. Do you think a sizable contribution to the theatre company could get the rehearsal schedules rearranged? After all, Lady Macbearth doesn't appear until Act I, Scene V. It will probably take a great deal of time for the three witches to get their act together and do all their prognostications."

"You know the play?"

"I guess I never told you about my short but highly charged acting career. And I'm not going to do it now. You're Bearyl's agent. You call and make them the offer."

"How much?"

"Don't go above five thousand. This trip is getting expensive with lawyer's fees, hotel damage repairs, hefty tips for bell-dogs, extra flights and contributions."

"You can afford it!"

"Of course I can afford it. I just don't like being taken advantage of."

While he checked in with the Colonel and the Frau, I went off in a corner and called the theatre director. After a little hemming, hawing and thanks for the contribution, Bearyl wouldn't be needed until next Thursday.

As I walked back, Condo and Otto sauntered in. I called Bearyl to tell her the news and got all kinds of: "Thank You; Thank you; Octavius is so wonderful; You're so wonderful; I'll feel much better with the Concorde back in its hangar; I better book a flight back from Abeardeen;" etc. etc. etc. Back to the issues at hand!

Both the wolves were getting pretty bored with their chaperone duties. They would be coming back shortly with their respective charges. Octavius told them to be available for our five o'clock session with Super Caballus.

Condo related the saga of the unworkable security system. When the name of Felicia Foxx came up, Octavius muttered one of his time-honored "Hmms"

"Ms Foxx seems to have been quite an active player in this little drama. That is, until her role was unexpectedly shortened. It would seem she was running interference for whomever got rid of Honoria and then played her last couple of moves rather poorly. Her involvement with the Opera fascinates me. I think we may have been spending too much of our time on the TV station and not enough on the Century Center. Have we interviewed everyone of the Opera's management team?"

"Everyone except the Director, Dr. Wolverine. The police probably spoke to him but I'd like to have a few moments with him myself."

"So would I, Maury. Let's make it a kind of courtesy call tomorrow. The singers' agent and one of their principal benefactors just stopping by. Felicia once worked for him didn't she? It seems Felicia piled up a long list of potential enemies in both places but I think her death was only collateral damage after the cow's murder. Maybe she threatened Honoria's killer with blackmail. She seemed arrogant and greedy enough to do it, well beyond the point of stupidity."

"Let's ask the RCUP to follow up on Manitoba Detection. They can probably get behind this security camera fiasco faster and more effectively than we can. Threats of lost licenses and all that. They can probably ferret out Ms Foxx's helpful relative quickly, especially with the help of Mr. Cody Coyote, ex of the RCUP and now of CWP-TV."

"I hope the local crime lab was able to get more information out of that wrench. Two different blood samples. Interesting! I wonder when Ottawa will get back with identifying those hairs found in Honoria's wounds."

"Do any of you have anything else to add? Facts? Opinions? Questions?"

"Just one," I said. "Do you expect any more information from Shetland Yard on Madame Honoria's money making activities? I can't believe her bank balance came strictly from voice coaching, especially since she was so lousy at it. I wonder who conned the Bearoness into using her."

"Knowing Superintendent Wardlaw's straight arrow personality, I'm sure he has shared all he currently knows with the RCUP. I'm not sure whether we will also be the beneficiaries of all that knowledge. Yes, I share your opinion that Madame Heifer was leading more than one professional life. Of course, we can't be sure there was anything illegal or immoral in those activities. The problem is I so disliked that cow that I could suspect her of practically anything. Anything else?"

Head shakes!

"Fine! We'll gather at five. I reserved a conference room on the mezzanine floor."

Chapter Twenty Seven

5 PM Thursday - The Ratison Hotel

Now it's time to exchange what we know.
Every detail retold blow-by blow.
Who (and why, when and how)
Killed the fox and the cow?
OK people, let's give it a go!

The Great Bear and I were the first to arrive in the conference room. It turned out that Octavius has arranged for dinner to be served as soon as we'd broken up this skull session. He doesn't mind spending money as long as it's his idea.

The door opened. A very bored Colonel Where shuffled in with the singers. Lepi and Bearnice looked truly beat. Tomorrow's full dress rehearsal with the orchestra won't help, either. I'm worried about their stamina for the two performances Sunday. Too late to change things now. Sales for the Sunday evening concert have been brisk. I'm sure Director Wolverine is pleased. Like most opera companies, The Manitoba is operating on a hand-to-mouth basis. These recitals came out of the blue from the Bearoness and are likely to raise the organization's staying power for a bit, at least. It will also provide our singers with a little independent cash for their own use. Given my own situation, I refused to consider asking for an agent's percentage. In fact, we don't really have a contract. I need to do something about that. I do have one with Otto. Again, no percentage.

Bearyl showed up with the Frau, beaming all over herself as she accepted congratulations and a big bear hug from Bearnice. She in turn, gave an embarrassed Octavius a gigantic embrace and licked his face, saying "Thank You" close to a hundred times. When she looked over at me, I just grabbed her paw and kissed it. Smallish meerkats can suffer badly from overly enthusiastic ursine squeezes.

After congratulating Bearyl, The Colonel and The Frau walked over to a corner of the room to get caught up with each other. Octavius lumbered over to them. "Before we get started, I have an assignment for both of you after dinner. Maury and I are going to drop in unannounced on Dr. Woodrow Wolverine, the Director of the Winnipeg Opera tomorrow. Find out anything you can about him. Personal and Professional! As far back as you can go. Get Chita in on this, too. That cat has all sorts of connections."

He had said the magic words. Madame Catt sauntered into the room with her photographer Fred. "Hi folks, I just want to get a few pictures of this happy band for background material. Then Fred will be leaving to take scenic shots of Winnipeg at night." Looking at Octavius, she winked and said, "I plan to stay. This whole affair fascinates me."

"Just as long as you remember that none of these discussions are for publication! None! Understand?"

"Gotcha, Bear!" The Queen of Sass replied. "But I want an exclusive interview with you after you tie it all up."

File that under Fat Chance. Let's see. We are missing Otto and Condo, Forrest Fox and of course, the star attraction, Superintendent Rowan Caballus of the RCUP. Otto came in next, did the congratulations gig with Bearyl and gave Lepi a high-five. He turned to Octavius and asked, "Are we still going to ask the Superintendent to follow up on Manitoba Detection?"

"You bet! Where's Condo?"

"Over here," said a disembodied voice in the center of the room.

"All right," growled the Bear, "Stop playing with that voice prosthetic and get in here."

The Condor came out from behind the curtains at the side of the room, flapped his wings, and saluted Bearyl with full Latin American grace and charm. "My felicitations, Senhorita Bearyl or should we start calling you Milady Macbearth."

"Bearyl is fine, Condo. Thank you!" She walked over to Bearnice and they began discussing how they were going to get the Flying Aquabear back to Abeardeen on Monday. Bearnice and Lepi would then go to Bearmoral Castle for a little R&R before heading off to Toronto. Next stop on their way to stardom.

I wondered if Chita wasn't just a bit jealous that Lepi, her old singing mate from the Spotted Band *(cf. Volume Two-The Case of the Spotted Band)* was now climbing the rungs of vocal prestige. As it was, she had teamed up with another member of the Band, a jaguar named Jake and occasionally cut loose in one London's many hot spots in her Catherine Catt guise. Speaking of a Hot Spot, that's the name of her oil rig in the North Sea. *(cf. Volume Three – A Case of Scotch)* A gift from a now dead admirer, the well was providing her with a steady income and leaving her with time to pursue her new editorial career. All told, a well established cat.

The only downsides were the arrest warrants from her Black Quack days with Imperius Drake, *(Moriarty with wings)* who may or may not have died in the cold waters of the Ohio River after an aerial duel with L. Condor. Chita had managed to elude the police who were showing decreasing interest in apprehending her. She was becoming increasingly bold in appearing where law enforcement roamed. Witness this evening's proximity to Superintendent Caballus. I'm not sure she's wanted for anything in Canada but just below the border was a different story. The United States is not a Chita-Friendly environment and her Madame Catherine Catt alias isn't foolproof by any means.

On cue, Super Caballus and Forrest Fox entered the room. Forrest was just winding up his report on Grigor Gregory as they came through the door and the Policeman seemed to buy it. Actually, if he wanted to pursue it, there was one flaw in the grizzly bear's alibi. He could account for his time when Felicia Foxx was killed but only loosely for the period covering Honoria's death. The current thinking was that both deaths were the responsibility of the same culprit and they gave Grigor the benefit of the doubt. *(doot)* It could still unravel.

They both congratulated Bearyl on her new role. The Super said, "It's a good thing we cleared you before today or we might have brought you back in for questioning as Lady Macbearth. *(Chuckle, chuckle)*

Octavius welcomed the two of them and invited them to stay for dinner. Both begged off. He turned to me and said, "Will you tell the manager there will be ten for dinner here in Conference Room C. Six o'clock should work. Thanks."

Messenger Meerkat to the house phone. Done and done! In the interest of fair play with the police, we went first with our reports. Otto and Condo did chapter, verse and footnotes on the CWP security system fiasco. The Super had known that the whole system was offline during both killings. What he didn't know was Felicia Foxx's possible involvement. Had she, through her as yet unidentified relative, managed to manipulate the installation schedules to coincide with Honoria's arrival? In short, was she aiding and abetting? Her involvement with the wrench seemed to be further proof. RCUP would follow up immediately with Manitoba Detection. The RCUP had several rounds with them in the past. They were not viewed as security vendor of the year.

We came next to the cow herself. What could the Scottish Police tell us aboot her other than she was a classic pain in the ass? Octavius and the Super combined their resources to come up with the following profile from Shetland Yard. Madame Heifer seems to have had a number of activities going on besides her coaching. First off, she was not based in Edinbeargh although she spent a lot of time there.

She first popped up in Germany where she ran a dating service. That's where she developed her skills in accumulating, analyzing and apparently, using scads of personal information from her clients and their "friends." She was accused several times of blackmail but no one seemed to be able to make the charges stick. She moved to England where she continued her "services" under different web-based titles and venues. She concentrated on the wealthy, powerful and popular. Her dating services were open to married as well as unmarried individuals who were interested mostly in dalliances rather than alliances.

A newspaper in Manchester ran a series of articles on her and she changed her name several times to avoid arrest or litigation. She knew very little aboot music but oddly for someone who wanted to remain out of the legal spotlight, she carried on her pretense of being a voice coach and former diva making public appearances right up until her death. Ego seems to have overcome common sense. The police consensus was she was murdered by one of her blackmail victims but she was so unpopular in other realms, her death might have been a simple act of unpremeditated anger. Given what seemed like an engineered setup by Felicia Foxx, that didn't seem very likely to any of us.

But our team and the police seemed to agree that the most likely suspects would come not from disgruntled singers but from strong and violent animals in the music or broadcast businesses with something very serious to lose. But who?

Next on the agenda, Ms Foxx. There seemed to be no question that she was complicit in Honoria's demise; arranging the interview on her own initiative; probably guiding her into the alley and her death; hiding the alleged weapon; arranging for the security camera system to be off-line. All in all, a very busy little Arctic Fox. And like Madame Heifer, not at all popular. There were, no doubt, quite a few animals quietly rejoicing at her passing. It was still possible that a different assailant did her in but the consensus was strongly against it.

Then we compared notes on our respective interviewees. Nobody stood out as Suspect Number One. On the contrary, the supply seemed to be running dry. The local crime lab could only say that the blood found on the head of the wrench belonged to Honoria and that the other blood, oddly on the handle, not the wrench head, seemed to be of the Mustelid or Ursine variety. Unfortunately, that covered just about every fur bearing species in Canada except cats. It wasn't even certain when that blood had gotten on the tool. Super Caballus had tried to stir the Ottawa labs to identify the hairs found in the cow's wounds and was assured it was being given high priority treatment. He snorted when he said that.

Finally, we mentioned that we planned an impromptu meeting with the Opera Director in the morning. Felicia Foxx had worked in his office. We asked the Super if he had any problem with that.

"No," he said, "although we did talk with him briefly. At the time, we weren't aware of the Felicia Foxx connection. He is one of Winnipeg's stellar citizens. Chairbeast of this charity, sponsor of that civic event, fund raiser extraordinaire and of course, leading light of the operatic scene, not only here but nationally. He said he had met Madame Heifer on one of her previous visits but had not seen her this trip. He was summarily unimpressed."

"Do you have any impressions you'd like to share, Forrest?"

"I can check with our commercial partners. I have no knowledge of any shady or criminal activities. Perhaps a political endorsement or two that shouldn't have been made but nothing extraordinary."

"Well," said Octavius, "it's probably a dead end but in the interest of completed staff work, Maury and I, agent and benefactor of the singers, will be paying a spontaneous courtesy call on him tomorrow. We'll keep you in the loop."

A door to the conference room opened and a waitress cat popped her head in, waiting to be invited to lay out the buffet. Octavius waved her in and said, "Looks like dinner is arriving. Are you sure you won't stay, Superintendent, Forrest? There should be plenty of excellent food. He looked at Frau Schuylkill for confirmation. The Frau had gone down to the kitchens and had no doubt created a small dustup with the hotel's culinary staff. She bowed at the great Bear. Once again, she was in command.

All that sustenance was going to be necessary as Chita, the wolves and I got ready for Operation Woodrow Wolverine. It was going to be a long night.

Chapter Twenty Eight

9 AM Friday - The Ratison Hotel

Taking time to precisely arrange
All the facts in our info exchange,
We can safely declare,
Even forcefully swear
The Director is certainly strange.

Scarfing down breakfast in Octavius' suite with Chita and the wolves. It was a strange night. We had divided up the task of tracking Dr. Woodrow Wolverine into separate segments: personal and family history; education; professional credentials; military history; social involvements; possible criminal and/or civil judgments; Winnipeg specific relationships and miscellany.

One fact came thundering out at us. If all of our researches, hasty though they were, are correct, Dr. Woodrow Wolverine didn't exist under that name earlier than ten years ago when he first emerged on the Winnipeg scene. Check, check and re-check.

Theories started to solidify. Assumptions emerged. Discussion accelerated. They all boiled down to two questions: Who the hell is this guy, really? Is he our killer?

Octavius, as usual, took the lead. "Let's not jump to conclusions just yet, although I admit it's very tempting. One of many items we overlooked, by the way, is just how formidable a predator a wolverine can be. They are famous for fighting and killing well above their weight and demonstrating a vicious personality in battle. Not as heavy as a bear, perhaps, but more than capable of subduing a cow."

Chita observed, "The connection between Honoria and the wolverine is probably wrapped up in her extra-curricular activities in, let's be polite, data gathering. I'm willing to bet she's been blackmailing him from a distance and when she returned to Winnipeg, he saw his opportunity to solve the problem permanently. For all of her cleverness in accumulating and capitalizing on personal scandals, she was awfully stupid or just too egotistical to believe she was in any danger from any of her victims. Felicia Foxx, no doubt, set up the killing for him and then decided to take advantage of the situation and engage in a little after the fact blackmail herself. What's the word? Hubris??"

The Great Bear responded, "Hubris and Greed! I'm inclined to agree. Now, tactical choices. Do we go ahead with our unannounced visit or not? When do we share our discoveries and theories with the police and how do we find out who Dr. Woodrow Wolverine really is? Let's remember, unless we are wildly out in left field, we have decided this could be one dangerous character."

My turn. "I think we should go ahead with our visit but include the Colonel, the Frau and Chita. Madame Catt can do her *PURR* and *SOW* magazine schtick. I doubt he would try anything violent with a nine foot tall bear, two wolves, a cheetah and, oh yes, a meerkat. I also think we should bring Otto and Condo up to speed in case we need their talents but keep them in reserve. I think we will have more to share with the RCUP after our visit."

The wolves and cat concurred. *(That hasn't happened very often.)*

Octavius said, "OK. Has everyone finished breakfast? Then, Colonel, how about getting out the vehicles and we'll go visit an Opera Director."

*****

The Opera was an exercise in choreographed confusion. Stagehands setting up lights, scrims and backdrops. Orchestra members filing into the pit, talking and testing their instruments. The Music Director and Orchestra Leader both bustling about, giving orders, explaining, disagreeing, agreeing, making notes and every thing else that makes a musical rehearsal so much fun.

The TV team was also working out camera and microphone placements, power supplies, angles and settings. Grigor was calmly weaving his way through the traffic, carrying a load of cables. He waved at us as we entered the auditorium. (*He didn't drop the cables.*)

The Colonel had joined Bearnice and Lepi back stage and was keeping an eye out for kindly Dr. Wolverine to make an appearance. Not yet. Probably leaving the confusion to his underlings. Otto and Condo were seated in the rear of the house near the steps to the executive wing. On call, if needed. The Frau was with us. She had decided Bearyl could get along without her for the time being.

So, with Octavius and I in the lead we made our way up to the Director's Office. His assistant, a smartly dressed and coiffed Red Fox vixen, *(He seems to have this thing about foxes.)* greeted us with some surprise. The

Great Bear has that effect. "Good morning, gentlebeasts. Are you here to see Dr. Wolverine?"

"Yes, we are," I said. "My name is Mauritius Meerkat and I represent Ms Bearnice Blanc and Mr. Leperello, the singers at this weekend's recitals. This is Dr. Octavius Bear, one of their primary benefactors. While we were here to view the dress rehearsal, we thought we might take the opportunity to pay a courtesy call on the Director. Ms Catt is the publisher-editor of two London based magazines, *PURR* and *SOW*. She is doing several major features on the concerts, the singers and this venue. Frau Ilse Schuylkill and Colonel Wyatt Where are our associates who are acting as bodyguards for the singers since the horrible murders this past week at the TV station."

The Fox shivered and said, "Yes, that was terrible. I don't suppose they have found who did it yet."

"Not to our knowledge," said the Bear.

"Well, I'm terribly sorry. I'm Viveca Vixen, Dr. Wolverine's assistant. Dr. Wolverine isn't here at the moment although I'm sure he would have been delighted to meet you. You are not unknown to us, Dr. Bear. Your generosity to the Arts is legendary."

"When do you expect him back?" I asked.

"I can't say for certain. He left me a voice mail saying he would be away from the office most of the day but he didn't say where he would be. That's unlike him. He is usually very conscientious about keeping me informed. Although he might have returned to the doctors. He seriously

177

injured his hind paw in a domestic accident earlier this week and it has been bothering him. But I really don't know. If he calls in, I will tell him you stopped by. Perhaps you can meet sometime over the weekend. I am so looking forward to attending the concert, myself. It's one of the perks of this job."

"Have you been with the Director long?" I asked.

"Just over two years. I replaced Felicia Foxx. She was the other murder victim, you know. She left to work at CWP-TV. I can't say I liked her much but what an awful thing to happen."

"Well," I said, "We'll be on the premises for the next several days and nights and would welcome a chance to say 'Hello!' Thanks so much for your help."

"My pleasure and may I say, Frau Schuylkill, how gorgeous you are. Such lovely fur!"

"Danke, Fraulein Vixen! You are hardly deficient in the beauty department, yourself. Your tail is magnificent."

The fox blushed and turned back to her computer as we turned away and made the trip downstairs.

"OK, now that the beauty show is over, let's see if we can find an empty and remote room to confer in."

I grabbed his paw. "Hey Octavius. That was totally insensitive and unnecessary. If the Bearoness was here, she would have cuffed you one. You owe the Frau an apology."

He looked at me in some amazement but then turned to the she-wolf and said, "My apologies, Frau Ilse *(Ilse!!)* I am just frustrated with how this whole thing is playing out. My manners need some polishing. You are, of course, a most attractive wolf."

I think that managed to keep the Colonel from telling him off. He smiled and gave me the lupine equivalent of the thumbs up.

We stepped back into the auditorium and I caught up with Godfrey, the Associate Director. I told him about stopping by the wolverine's office but he was a no-show.

The goose said, "He's been in and out more than usual over the last several days. Strange with sell-out shows coming up. He's usually all over us. I know his foot has been bothering him. Some kind of accident. Not sure what. Anyway, we have everything under control and that third concert is selling very well. Thanks for your help on that."

I asked him if there was a room we could use for an hour or so and he gave me a key to a rehearsal space on the basement floor.

Present: Octavius, Frau Schuylkill, Colonel Where, Chita, Otto, Condo and yours truly.

I was feeling unusually aggressive this morning. Maybe it was the result of chiding The Great Bear. Anyhow, I started the conversation, "I think it's time we teamed up with Superintendent Caballus again. Share and share alike, if he's willing. There are too many loose ends here. Who is the wolverine, really? What was his connection with Honoria? Was she blackmailing him or threatening him some other way? Is he the killer? Did Felicia stage manage the event and then end up being murdered herself? What's with the wound the wolverine is supposed to have. Does that explain the second bloodstain on the wrench? If he did kill them both, what's the motive? Probably has something to do with his life before Winnipeg. Where is he now? Did he skip town?"

I ran out of breath.

"Not a bad menu, Meerkat," said the Bear. "I agree. We need to tie in with the police. Not here! If Caballus showed up in the Center, suspicions would rise up all over the place. Maybe we ought to meet him on his turf. Any objections? *(Octavius was being awfully democratic lately. Interesting!)* OK, I'll call!"

"Superintendent Caballus, please. Rowan? Octavius! Look, I think it's time we put our heads together on these murders. We have a lot of facts and theories we want to share with you and we're hoping you have some information you can contribute to us. How about your office at one o'clock? Fine! We'll grab an early lunch and meet you there. Who am I bringing? Oh, just the usual suspects."

He turned to us and said, "Let's sort out today's lineup. Colonel, I hate to ask this of you but I'd like you to stay here with Lepi and Bearnice. The Opera staff is used to seeing you and they may, in fact, wonder if you're not around. However, what I really want you to do is keep watch for the wolverine's return. Let us know the minute he shows, if he shows. Chita, I think it would be wise if you didn't march into police headquarters. Caballus doesn't seem to know you as Madame Catherine but someone else might. *(The cat agreed.)* Frau Schuylkill, how would you like to take Ms Vixen to lunch, compare beauty secrets and give your investigative skills an outing? Otto, Maury, Condo and I will descend on the RCUP."

And so it began! Since there wasn't a driver in the bunch going to RCUP, the colonel drove us over and then returned to the Opera. Meanwhile the Frau kept watch for the wolverine's arrival. No show. The Music Director called a lunch break just as the Colonel came back. He came over to Bearnice and Lepi. "How's it going?" he asked,

"Pretty smoothly. You know, The Edinbeargh Opera could learn a few things from these folks. That recital had its nightmarish moments. Of course, Honoria was there to add to the chaos. But we survived it."

"You bet you did. You were a smash. If the Scots thought you were great these enthusiastic Canadians will fall all over you. I can just see Kitty and Maxie on their feet whistling and hooting."

"Aren't they great?" said Bearnice, "We included the Indian Love Howl in the program just for them. It won't sound quite the same without a couple of bowls of liquor to oil the engine but what the heck."

"Look," said Wyatt. "I have a favor to ask of you. We've been trying to get together with Director Wolverine but so far he's proven pretty elusive. I don't know whether he's ducking us or is just unavailable, period. Anyway, I'm on the lookout for him and if you spot him, let me know. Don't stop anything. Just signal me if you can."

"We can't see out in the Auditorium with the lights shining in our faces but if he shows backstage or in the wings, we'll let you know."

"Don't worry. I've got the auditorium covered as well as the stairs to the executive wing. Speaking of the executive wing, there's Ilse over there with the Director's Assistant, Ms Vixen. I guess she took the Frau up on her lunch invitation. Ilse's pretty good at drawing out information from unsuspecting companions. We'll see what she comes up with.

*****

"Once again, Frau Vixen. It is Frau, is it not?"

"Oh yes, I am happily mated with two kits."

"Ah! I myself am divorced. A long ago story. But anyway, once again I truly want to congratulate you on your lovely appearance. Quite extraordinary!"

"Thank you. Coming from a beauty like you, that is quite a compliment."

"But sincerely meant."

"Well, being the Director's Assistant requires me to make a good impression on the many visitors he receives. Appearance is only part of it, of course, but it is an important part. He belongs to so many local and regional associations and even a national commission. He claims that I represent his office as well as he does and he insists that we maintain a high standard of professionalism and decorum. Between us, I think that's what made Felicia Foxx quit. I hate to use the word but she was so 'common' if you know what I mean. I expect you have the same demanding situation. Dr. Bear seems to be a creature of very high standards."

The Frau chuckled inwardly and thought, "You don't know the half of it."

"Oh ja, Frau Vixen, but being in the employ of Herr Bear is most rewarding. I wouldn't trade my career for anything although I have been made some attractive offers from time to time. He is a very unique animal and his staff and associates are quite remarkable. I assume you know that in addition to his wonderful inventions, businesses, charities and worldwide organizations, we spend some of our time in the solution of crimes and the capture of criminals. That is most exciting. For example, since Madame Heifer was an employee of his mate, The Bearoness Belinda Béarnaise Bruin Bear (nee Black), he has taken it upon himself to assist the police in tracking down the murderer or murderers. He has an extraordinary record of success in bringing wrongdoers to justice. But enough of me and Herr Bear. Tell me more about you and the Director. Is he married?"

"Now, you are going to think this very strange but I don't know. If he is mated, he is living apart.

"Where does he live?"

"Somewhere in the Exchange District, I think. In fact, I know very little about him personally and only what is published in his Curriculum Vitae about his professional background. He is a very private creature. I do know he came to Winnipeg about ten years ago and rapidly rose to his current position. I was not on staff during most of that time. I was hired as an assistant to one of the business managers and I responded to a posting for this job after Felicia Foxx left. I'm not even sure where he came from before joining the Opera. His résumé mentions Germany and England but no dates."

"Germany and England," thought Frau Schuylkill, "just like our late unlamented friend, Honoria Heifer."

Aloud "That is strange but his credentials and references must have been more than sufficient to land him this job."

"Oh, I'm sure that's true. Now where would you like to eat? There's a nice, reasonable trattoria in the next block. Do you like Italian food?"

The cordon bleu chef replied, "My favorite!"

Chapter Twenty Nine

10:30 AM Friday – RCUP Headquarters

The researchers from RCUP
Have uncovered a deep mystery.
They don't know but somehow
The Director and cow
Have a very short life history.

Otto, Condo, Octavius and I took seats at one side of a badly scuffed conference table and Superintendent Caballus took up a good part of the other side along with two Pocket Gophers, each armed with a tablet computer.

"These two officers are the mainstays of our Research Division. Sergeants Gough and Geoffrey. They have been doing in-depth background checks on Honoria Heifer and Felicia Foxx. They have some interesting material for you."

"Before we launch into that, Rowan, I wonder if I could ask them to do further research on Dr. Woodrow Wolverine, as well. We haven't paid much attention to him but we have come to the conclusion that he might be a most interesting person of interest."

"We're on him, Octavius. In retrospect, his arrival in Winnipeg was rather strange. It's almost as if he suddenly arrived from outer space."

"Oh, I doubt he's an extraterrestrial but there does seem to be something alien about him. We've been trying to get an audience with him and we've had no luck at all. Frau Schuylkill is schmoozing with his assistant over lunch. We'll see what she comes up with. Meanwhile, back to the cow and arctic fox."

Sergeant Gough piped up, "I've been pursuing Honoria and Geoffrey here has been on Felicia Foxx. I assume you've been doing your own research as well. Let's compare notes. We're pretty sure Madame Heifer has been in the, shall we say, international dating service business for quite a while. That sort of thing can lead to all sorts of sidelines and based on our searches of her clients, it certainly did. In fact, we believe she was a one-animal vice ring with a good chunk of blackmail tossed in."

Octavius rumbled, "That's what we concluded. Unfortunately, that opens up the list of suspects to a pretty wide range of individuals, unless, as we are beginning to believe, she was somehow connected with our friend, the wolverine. In our searches for animals big enough and strong enough to kill off a large cow, we overlooked the impressive killer qualities of an aggressive wolverine. By the way, have you heard from Ottawa on those hairs the medical examiner found?"

"They're promising us results later in the day. I'll believe it when I see it."

I intervened, "According to the Opera staff, Dr. Wolverine has been suffering for the last several days from some sort of problem with one of his hind legs. The medical examiner did say the blood type found in the second

186

stain on the wrench could belong to a wolverine as well as a lot of other species. If it's a wound, he may have gone to a doctor or medical facility for treatment."

"Thanks, Maury! Get on that one, Geoffrey!" said Caballus. "If he's guilty, he may be toughing it out with self treatment. But he may also believe he is above suspicion and is simply going about his business with an accidental wound treated by a doctor or nurse. In that case, we might get something back from a medical search. Do you think his assistant would know?"

"We'll find out when the Frau calls in. Meanwhile what more do we know about Felicia?"

Geoffrey read from his notes. "She was a real climber both at the Opera and CWP. Not really well liked in either place. Took to bossing people around at the Opera using her position as the Director's assistant to get what she wanted. Not exactly sure why she left the Opera. The job at CWP paid more but was much further down the pecking order. But it's likely she had a plan to change all that. If Dr. Wolverine did indeed knock off the cow, we could probably make a case for him doing the same thing to Ms Foxx. But the list of animals who had her on their "Least Popular" list is pretty long and even though it's a long shot, the killings maybe unrelated."

Octavius replied, "I don't believe that for a moment. Too many coincidences to contend with. I think Otto's discovery of her hiding the murder weapon ties her directly to the cow's killer."

"Actually, we believe that, too." said Geoffrey, We've checked her home; *(a small downtown apartment)* friends; *(she didn't have many)* her hangouts; *(a couple of bars)* and her life style. That's where the profile gets interesting. She drove an expensive sports car, had an extensive wardrobe and enough jewelry to open a store. She obviously had another source of income besides her salary from the TV station. Maybe several sources. Her credit cards show some pretty large expenditures but she paid them off every month. She took a couple of trips to the States and overseas. Germany and England."

"Germany and England!" I interrupted, "Honoria's stomping grounds. Do we know where she went in those countries?"

"Munich and Manchester among others!"

"Where was Honoria before she came to Edinbeargh?"

"Munich and Manchester!"

"Why is my nose tickling? Do I sense a certain symmetry here? Is there a confluence of places and events that may just have a bearing on this whole megillah? Don't let the subtlety elude us."

"Sarcasm is not your strong suit, Meerkat." muttered Octavius. "He's right, though. Let's see what links we can establish between those two. It might also explain how Felicia set up the TV interview without anyone else's involvement. She and Honoria had been working together. But then it looks like the cow became dispensable. I really want to talk to the Opera Director. He's a key in this thing. I wonder what news, if any, the Frau has."

(Employing, once again, the wonders of convenient narrative ploys, his phone rang. Frau Ilse Schuylkill on the line. You're not surprised, are you?)

"Bear here! Hello Frau. Any news? Well, he's certainly making himself scarce. With the recitals coming up tomorrow and Sunday, I would have thought he'd be micro-managing the whole process. Has his assistant been any help at all? He lives in the Exchange District? *(Octavius waved at the gophers.)* OK, we'll follow up on that. What about this mysterious wound he seems to be nursing? No details! He doesn't seem to keep her in the loop, does he? When did he arrive in Winnipeg? Ten years or so. Did you get a copy of his Curriculum Vitae? Good! Where did he come from? Germany and then England? *(Dramatic organ music in the background. Just kidding!)* OK, we'll be wrapping up here at headquarters pretty shortly. Meet us at the Century Center. I still have the key Godfrey gave us for the conference room. Get a hold of the Colonel when you arrive. Thanks. What? You don't like Canadian-Italian food. Sorry, I owe you one."

He turned to the Super. "Do you agree with me that we need to get our respective appendages on Dr. Woodrow Wolverine ASAP? I'm still not sure how any of this is going to play out but our information sources seem to be all pointing in the same direction."

"I'm going to start by getting on Ottawa's back about those hairs in the wound. The blood stains on the wrench didn't tell us enough. Of course, if we can get a hold of him, we can match the DNA but as you say, first we have to get a hold of him. This triangle sounds like everyone was playing against each other. You have to wonder whether there are anymore participants in the game. Let us know immediately if he shows up at the Opera."

"I doubt he has. Both Frau Schuylkill and Colonel Where have the place under surveillance. Not much gets past them."

Chapter Thirty

2 PM Friday – Winnipeg Opera

The Director's eluding us still
And he's using exceptional skill.
We're beginning to doubt
We can make him come out.
I'm not betting that we ever will.

Back in the rehearsal room. Present: Octavius, Frau Schuylkill, Colonel Where, Otto, Condo and me, the meerkat. Lepi and Bearnice were working through the program with the orchestra and the TV crew. Chita and Bearyl were together in the back of the auditorium along with Chita's photographer, Fred plotting out stories and photo spreads.

"Otto, can you spell the colonel on his wolverine watch. Colonel, have you had any lunch?"

"No problem, Octavius."

"Actually, I'd like Otto on watch for a while. If the wolverine's assistant leaves early, I'd like you, Otto, to scout out the contents of his office. If not, we'll do it later tonight after the house has gone dark. One thing I'd like to know is where the box office receipts are stored over the weekend. Take a look in his desk for anything that might indicate travel plans. Look especially for places his assistant might not have access to. I have a sneaking suspicion our Director friend may be planning a disappearing act."

"The RCUP have also turned their attention to the Director," said Octavius. "There seems to be a link between our subjects and the cities of Munich and Manchester. I'm hoping we can dig up sufficient evidence to place them all together at one time in either or both of those cities. Are we having any luck tying anything up yet?"

"Maybe we should call Shetland Yard again," I proposed. "Super Wardlaw may be able to scare up some more information through Interpol and Scotland Yard."

"Good idea, Maury. Get on the phone with him and let's see if we can fill in a few more blanks."

Meanwhile Otto had left the room. *(In conventional style. You never know who you'll startle if you suddenly pop up out of nowhere.)* He made his way up the executive stairs just in time to see Viveca Vixen locking up her desk and preparing to leave. An early evening with her mate and kits, no doubt. He skittered down the stairs and waited for her to head out the door. Then, he zapped into the Director's office unobserved by anyone including the wolverine who was sitting at his desk poring over some files. Time for a hasty and hopefully, unseen retreat. "How the hell did he get past our surveillance? How long has he been here? What's he doing?"

A quick zap down to the rehearsal room. "He's here," Otto blurted, "and it looks like he's been in his office for a while. He has files spread out all over his desk. I don't think he saw me. I popped in and out without him looking up. His assistant has left for the day. I'm not sure she knew he was in there. The door was locked. There must be another way into that office. Maybe through an adjacent bathroom. He may share the loo with his Associate Director who's been down in the auditorium most of the day. But we should have seen him come in that way, too. Do you want to go up and face him down now?"

"I don't think so," said the Great Bear. "We can't claim we're making a social call on him if he's locked in his office and we don't have enough solid proof of anything to storm the bastions. Call Super Caballus, Maury, and tell him we have found the wolverine. Let's see what he wants to do. He can always pull the 'person of interest' routine on him. We can't. Otto, go back up there and see if you can figure out how he slipped into his office."

The otter zapped into the Associate Director's office and looked around for an adjoining door or joint access to a bathroom. Nothing. One theory shot to hell. Unless! Suppose he just waited until Viveca Vixen went out to lunch with the Frau, came down, disguised as someone else who belonged in the Executive wing and slipped into his office while no one was looking. Probably dressed as a female or a maintenance worker that no one would notice. This place is awash in costumes and makeup. He could probably leave the same way. No secret doors or hidden elevators. That stuff belongs in Bearmoral Castle with the Bearoness. Back to the rehearsal room.

While Otto explained his theory, the colonel re-entered the room after getting a snack. Octavius asked him, "Colonel, did you see anyone else enter or leave by the Executive Stairs while you were there?"

"Sure, there was a fair amount of traffic up and down those halls and stairways. With a show like this in progress, you'd expect that but he didn't show."

"Not looking like himself, he didn't." said Otto. "I'm willing to bet he came in here in disguise. He's up in his office now. I almost zapped in on top of him."

"One must ask," said Condo, "why the Director of the Opera is in need of a disguise in his own domain. Or is he trying out for the Phantom of the Opera?"

"He may be trying to evade a jail cell. He's getting ready to fade into the sunset. What's holding him up?"

The Frau spoke up, "Money. Three shows this weekend. Remember how excited he was about doing that third show on Sunday. Box office cash locked up in a safe somewhere. Let's talk to the Associate Director and find out how they handle that. They could use a night depository or they may just wait until Monday morning."

Octavius looked at Otto. "Can you get into that bathroom and keep tabs on him without being noticed?

"I may have to make a fast getaway but, sure, I can do that."

Off went Otto. Quick entry into the bathroom. Peeking out at the Director. Problem: No Director. "He must have left while I was down below," thought the otter.

He ran out onto the Executive stairway and caught a glimpse of an animal in coveralls carrying a stack of costumes. He zapped up behind the costume bearer and deliberately tumbled into him. On the floor in a tangle of clothes. His target got up slowly and stared at the otter, "What the hell? Boy, are you clumsy! You could have pushed me down the entire staircase. What's the big hurry, shorty? You help me pick this stuff up."

"Gee, I'm sorry. I was in a hurry and I tripped. Are you OK?"

"Yeah, I'm OK."

He may have been OK but one thing was clear. This animal was no wolverine. He was an oversized skunk. Let's hope he doesn't get too angry. After picking up and refolding the clothes while apologizing every five seconds Otto said, "I didn't expect to see anyone carrying a stack of clothes moving down the Executive Corridor."

"It's a quick shortcut from backstage to the shops and wardrobe rooms. Some of the bosses get angry about us using it but they use it, too. I passed the Director on my way through here just a minute ago."

"I guess it's an easy exit from the building."

"Yeah, if you know your way around backstage."

An "Aha Moment!" Back to the rehearsal room.

*****

Superintendent Caballus *(in plain clothes)* had joined the group. He snorted while Otto described what had happened. "Well, he's gone for the moment." I didn't pass him on the way in so he, no doubt, took that stage exit and is off somewhere. We have his flat under surveillance. Otto, can you go up and do a quick inventory of the office? You say he had a lot of files he was going through the first time you zoomed in there. Want to bet he took some of them with him and also pushed a bunch of them through his office shredder? This guy is acting more and more guilty by the minute. But what the hell was his motive. I'm issuing an 'all points bulletin' on him.

Chapter Thirty One

3PM Friday – Winnipeg Opera

We have evidence building up fast
Of the wolverine's criminal past.
And his partner, the cow.
We are plotting out how
We can finally nab him at last

While Otto was rummaging through the Director's office, I was on the horn with Shetland Yard. Superintendent Wardlaw was working overtime on this one for us. The RCUP and Octavius owe him one. A few items had surfaced that were thickening the plot. First was the unsolved disappearance about twelve years ago in Munich of a musical impresario named ***Werner Wolverine.*** The German Polizei have no record of a ***Woodrow Wolverine***.

It seems Werner had a very profitable booking agency that specialized in bringing young classically trained talent into the concert milieu. There were also suspicions that Werner's booking activities were not limited to musical harmony. Other congenial services seemed to be available to select clientele through a companion organization run by a rather notorious bovine named ***Hermione Heifer***. Then suddenly the whole operation folded its tents in a hurry leaving a host of musical hopefuls and several major concert venues high and dry. The polizei also theorize that a number of pleasure oriented, well-to-do clients lost a major resource and probably significant euros paid in membership fees and future bookings. Interviews with Werner's protégés produced nothing of significance. Several of them could not be found for questioning.

No one seems to have connected the dots when Woodrow Wolverine surfaced in Manchester about two years later along with then Honoria Heifer. They probably chose Manchester to maintain a certain amount of anonymity. Too many questions could be asked in London. Alas for them, a conflict with other "booking" services made their stay in Manchester short-lived. This time they split up. Honoria moving to Edinbeargh and Woodrow to Winnipeg.

The RCUP came up with the following: By falsifying records and extorting cooperation out of several of their former European pleasure clients, they each were able to build a set of credentials that could stand up to none too careful scrutiny. It took Woodrow a year or two of finagling, schmoozing, pressuring, bribing, lying, back scratching, threatening and other social niceties to land the Director's job. He knew enough about the musical world to carry off the deceit.

Honoria simply re-invented herself, restarted her "matching" agency in Edinbeargh and then, in a burst of pure chutzpah, decided to pass herself off as a vocal coach as well. Woodrow helped by providing her with phony references from the musical world and gave her a short course in coaching. Clearly, the references looked strong enough to convince even a worldly wise and show biz experienced individual like Bearoness Belinda Béarnaise that her bona fides were acceptable enough to put Bearnice and Lepi under her tutelage. As our singers' experience so powerfully illustrated, she was a lousy coach who lost clients by the dozens. It is probably a good thing the Bearoness is in gestation hibernation or she might have killed Honoria herself by this time.

But what led to the double murder? Woodrow Wolverine tops everyone's list as the prime suspect but the circumstances, motive and the involvement of Felicia Foxx all remain a mystery.

*****

Meanwhile, back in the Director's office, Otto was working his magic on desk and closet locks. The shredder, full to capacity was a lost cause. The RCUP might be able to recover something in their labs. He was surprised the Director hadn't emptied it and taken the slivers with him. One conclusion: He might be coming back.

The wolverine had done a pretty comprehensive job of eliminating anything that might have use as evidence against him. No personal or personnel material. No lists of contacts or contracts. No personal computer or PDA. The only paper files left were the sort most of the Opera's management might also have as copies. Schedules, events, copies of speeches, newspaper and magazine articles. Public domain stuff. All of his desktop clutter was still there. Paper weights, citations, photos with VIPs and Opera stars. You had to look carefully to notice that this office that looked like it was still in use was functionally empty. Woodrow Wolverine seemed experienced in the fine art of getaway.

*****

Meanwhile Frau Schuylkill had stopped by the office of Godfrey Gander, the Opera's Associate Director. She was fully aware that right next door, Otto was having his way with the contents of the Director's office. Godfrey's assistant waved the she-wolf into his office.

"Ah, Frau Schuylkill, how nice to see you. What service can I perform for you? More tickets?"

"Oh, nein, Herr Gander. It is kind of you to offer. Perhaps you could satisfy a bit of personal curiosity, though. You see, I have been in the employ of Herr Dr. Octavius Bear for quite a few years and in that time, in addition to being his personal cook, chief pilot, housekeeper and security officer, I have often helped him in his investigations. I also, along with Colonel Wyatt Where, make recommendations to our clients about improving their security and establishing precautions against breaking and entering, theft, personal assault and the like. One thing I have often noticed is how lop-sided some organizations are when it comes to protective measures. For example, we just discovered that CWP, with all of their security detection equipment installed, had actually taken it down for upgrades and went for several days without any back-up processes."

Godfrey gulped, "Is that when the murders took place?"

"Exactly! How perceptive of you. We think the murderer or murderers was well aware of this and took full advantage of it. I am not aware of any security detection equipment here at the Center."

"I hate to admit it but there isn't any to speak of. The Center is, of course, managed by a separate team and while we occupy a number of offices and facilities, we are essentially tenants subject to the decisions of the Center's management. I must confess, though, that security has never been very high on our lists of concerns. Oh, we worry about safety. Any theater can be an accident prone environment and we and the Center's management are quite insistent on keeping physical controls on all hazards. Our fire and water alarm systems are state of the art. But when it comes to the sort of security I think you're talking about, we are pretty lax."

"Let me give you an example. Recently, Ms Bearnice and Mr. Leperello gave a recital at the Edinbeargh Opera House. After the performance, an attempt was made on the life of Bearoness Belinda Béarnaise Bruin *(nee Black, now Bear)*. Fortunately, we foiled it. But there were no scanners or searchers at the entries to the auditorium and the would be killer got through carrying a weapon. *(The Frau neglected to add that she and the colonel also got through carrying weapons.)*

"My goodness," said the goose, "Mayhem seems to follow those two around."

"I certainly hope not," said the Frau, "but we discovered another thing while were there. The house receipts were shamefully unprotected. They were simply locked in a till inside a locked box office. Very vulnerable!"

"Now," replied the gander, "We're one up on that subject. At the end of a performance, the receipts are gathered up in separate bags for cash, credit and debit cards and checks and taken up to the Director's office and stored in his safe until the next morning when the armored truck comes by. Only the cashier, the Director and I have the combination to the safe. So, even over a weekend, our proceeds are protected."

The Frau simply nodded. As they say, "The penny dropped."

*****

The rehearsal had just broken up in the auditorium and our team emerged from the downstairs meeting room to greet the weary performers. The Music Director and Orchestra Leader were both gushing all over themselves with compliments and congratulations. The TV group said they were satisfied and ready for tomorrow night's opening. The Associate Director arrived to add his "well dones." As expected by us at least, the Director was nowhere to be seen. No one mentioned the absence. We all joined in the virtual back slapping. Bearyl had arrived to join the group. Octavius announced that he had arranged a post-rehearsal dinner for all and invited the Opera group to join us. When the Orchestra Leader and Music Director begged off, the Associate Director Gander allowed as how he would represent the establishment. Still no comment on the wolverine's absence. Superintendent Caballus claimed pressing business elsewhere. Before he left, Octavius took him, Otto, the Frau and myself aside.

"What did you find?" he asked Otto.

"It's what I didn't find." said the otter, "He has systematically emptied or shredded all of his important files. His computer and associated discs are gone. He left the office looking occupied. I opened the safe in his office closet. Empty! I came down to get a bag so I can collect the contents of the shredder. Do you want it, Superintendent?"

"Yes! We have a couple of techies on our staff who can reassemble shredded documents provided they're not too badly torn up."

"OK," said Otto, "I'll be right back." Zap!!

"I've seen him do that before but it still amazes me."

"It amazes us, too," said The Bear. "I think he's still amazed by it."

The Frau looked at them and said, "That safe may be empty now but by Sunday night it will be filled with the weekend's receipts waiting for the armored car on Monday morning. The cashier; Herr Gander the Associate Director; and our friend, the Wolverine are the only ones who have the combination. *(and Otto, of course.)* I am willing to bet he will be back in that office late Sunday night to make off with the money to finance another one of his rapid getaways."

"Not if we get to him first. He hasn't been near his apartment and we have an APB out for him. If you're right, Frau Schuylkill, he must be still in the area. If not, he must have left town on the back roads. I wonder if he can drive with that wounded leg. There has been no sign of him at the airport, train or bus stations. We've also checked the taxi and van services. If he tries to cross the border into the States, we'll probably get him."

"I hope you're right, Superintendent. Remember, he's pretty experienced in the art of the fast disappearance."

203

"True, Octavius, true! But we're no slouches. Remember our motto. 'We always get our animal!'"

Otto zapped back into the room with several plastic bags filled with paper shards. "Here you are, Superintendent. I hope you can get something out of them."

"Before you leave, Rowan, one more subject. Felicia Foxx! Do we have any better idea of how she fits into all this? We can make a pretty good guess, of course but her visits to Munich and Manchester puzzle me."

I piped up. "She made those trips after the wolverine arrived here in Winnipeg and Honoria went to Edinbeargh. I checked the data that Shetland Yard sent us from Scotland Yard. I'm not even sure why they know about her. Sounds like she may have been doing some independent investigating on her own but what made her suspicious in the first place? And what made Scotland Yard suspicious of her?"

"Do we know when Honoria made her first visit to Winnipeg?" asked Octavius. "She's been here several times, supposedly on coaching trips with her protégés. If Felicia was still the wolverine's assistant, she may have overheard some conversations between him and the cow and saw an opportunity for applying pressure."

"The Director's assistant, Ms Vixen, may know the dates if they archive their calendars. I'll check." said the Frau. "Ach, she may have gone home. If she did, I know she's coming to one of the performances. Maybe I can talk to her then."

Chapter Thirty Two

3:30 PM Saturday – Winnipeg Opera

That's Octavius out on that limb.
It's a funny position for him.

He believes that he's right
And he certainly might.
He's not thinking this up on a whim.

As soon as the Superintendent left, Octavius turned to the rest of us and said, "My nose is twitching. Let's get Howard on the phone."

The Frau smiled, I dialed and Otto look confused.

"Howard? Maury! Fine, fine. The kids are just about ready for their big night. Just a few more hours. I assume you know about the murders. Murders plural! First the cow and then an arctic fox who seems to have been tied up in it and got herself killed. Practically the same M.O. Look, Octavius wants to talk with you. The Frau, Otto and I are here too. Can you patch us all in on our cell phones so we can have a group conversation? OK. Set up the number and we'll all dial in."

I looked over at Octavius who was getting antsy. No toleration for techie trifling. Howard came back, gave us the number and we all dialed in including the Great Bear.

"Howard? Look, we have some rather peculiar things going on right now and I'm beginning to think a bit of universe shifting may be happening. Have you made much progress in the last few days? A possible breakthrough? Well, that's the first encouraging thing I've heard all day."

(Everybody's on! I shall now reproduce for you the five-way conversation.)

"You may or may not think it's encouraging, Octavius. The evidence is piling up. We're getting isolated reports from a number of sources. I don't think anyone else has picked up on the total picture yet. Maybe General Turmoil and his bunch have but you're not going to hear from them until it's probably too late. I can validate several hundred incidents and there are a lot more fragmentary items. Very few repeats but they seem to break down into four general categories or universe types."

Octavius interrupted, "Wait a minute, Howard. I want the colonel on this call. After all, he's the one in our group who's had the most personal experience with this. Can you fetch him, Frau?"

(Silly question. I decided to time how long it would take for the other wolf to be in with us. Octavius started to fill the time by telling Howard what had transpired and the strange behavior of Woodrow (Werner) Wolverine. He got about three sentences out and the two wolves were in the room. "Höchstgeschwindigkeit" hyperspeed! Forty seconds. Slow but she had to find him first! Dialing up – another twenty seconds.)

"OK, Howard, we're all on board and listening avidly."

"Hi, Wyatt. I was just telling the group that I think, based on the evidence we have accumulated so far there are four major types of alternate universes, including us. I'm sure there are variants but let's keep it simple."

(All we're talking about is restructuring the cosmos, so by all means let's keep it simple.)

"By the way, Marlin did a great job massaging a lot of this data. We need to keep him around, Octavius."

"The Prince of Whales expects him and a supply of undersea voice translators back ASAP, Howard. I'll have to fulfill that promise before we start negotiating for a dolphin aquatic team member. Anyway, what have you come up with?"

"As I said, for the moment, I've extracted only two very basic characteristics of interest to us: The presence or absence of H.Saps and the presence or absence of Advanced Animals approximately like us. There are many other distinctions that will bear on our further research and decision making. For example, if H.Saps, Advanced Animals or both exist in a world, how far advanced are they measured against us? In the hundreds of examples we've managed to unearth, *(bad pun)* we often don't have enough evidence to make that call. The presence or absence of language, tools, social organization, infrastructure, communication and the like may give us hints but I'm currently of the opinion that among all of these worlds there as many differences as there are similarities. It's not clear, for instance, whether the Great Shock took place in all of them and if so what impact it had."

"I am operating on an assumption that these alternate universes are virtually separated, not physically separated. Remember, we're talking about quantum superposition of all possible alternatives in the same space. We're not physically traveling through the cosmos to other galaxies. We're tussling with quantum mechanics right in our own backyard."

(I'm glad we're keeping to the simple version.)

"I think our first order of business is trying to determine where threats to our Earth are most likely to develop. Let's lay it out graphically. On your screens, you can see a four by two grid, vastly oversimplified. I've given each class of universe a name starting with ours.

		H.Saps	Advanced Animals
1.	Earth (Us)	No	Yes
2.	Terra (Colonel)	Yes	No
3.	World (Juno)	No	No
4.	Gaea (Agrippa)	Yes	Yes

Universes 2 and 4 are of most interest to us and I'm concentrating on them. Colonel, in your trips to Terra, have you ever encountered animals at or above our level of intelligence?"

"First off, Howard, I'm not sure I have always been going to the same place although it is becoming increasingly familiar. But to answer your question, the animals I've encountered are often intelligent in a feral way but haven't attained anywhere near the level of development that we have. The

H.Saps, on the other hand, are right up there with us on the advancement scale, maybe even ahead of us. It's tough to measure strictly from anecdotes and spotty observation."

Octavius interrupted, "Let's remember one thing. If H.Saps showed up here on Earth, they'd stick out like sore paws provided they weren't in disguise. That's pretty tough to manage. The universe that interests me is number 4, Gaea. From Agrippa's story about the poker game he was dealing, H. Saps and Advanced Animals seemed to co-exist and cooperate there, even if the game did end up in a shoot-out. If we are going to concentrate on possible threats to our Earth, that's the place *(or places)* that's the most likely candidate. Howard, I'm operating on an extremely wild theory that right here in Winnipeg we may be dealing with a few Advanced Animals from another universe."

Otto and I gulped in unison. The Frau and the Colonel looked at each other, smiled and nodded.

"We have several intelligent animals who just showed up seemingly out of the blue about ten years ago in Germany, moved to England and then here. I admit that's pretty flimsy evidence by itself but they don't pass my intuitive sniff test."

(Octavius holds great store on his intuitive sniff tests. The trouble is he's almost always right.)

"One of them is, was, Honoria Heifer and another is the Director of this Opera Company, Woodrow or Werner Wolverine. There may be a couple of others. I'd like you to work from the other end and see if you can uncover anything that would support my theory. I think, if the denizens of Gaea exist at all, they, like us, may only have a few Multiverse travelers. If there are adepts among their H.Saps and Advanced Animals, it's likely they'd send the animal versions to our world. They'd blend in while the H.Saps wouldn't"

I piped up. "Octavius, isn't it just possible that you're letting this Multiverse thing run away with your judgment. You're the great advocate of choosing the simplest solution to any problem. I think we need to exhaust some more conventional theories on these murders before we go to quantum land."

"Absolutely, Maury. We must keep this idea on the back burner. Under no circumstances should we mention it to the authorities. I do want to bring L. Condor up to speed on this, however. He has a mind that can pick its way through bits and pieces of evidence and come up with plausible patterns. Colonel, can you brief him on our discussions? I assume you and the Frau are open to further exploring my theory."

"You bet, Octavius, although I share Maury's feelings about following the more prosaic paths as well."

"Frau Schuykill, what do you think?"

"I think it is possible, Herr Bear, but I think we need a great deal more evidence before we jump to conclusions. It is very unusual, however, the way they seemed to pop up from out of nowhere. If they are from Gaea or wherever, why are they here? Are they some kind of scouts? Maybe they're fugitives. They don't seem to be trying to establish formal contact with any authorities or experts. If you do finally meet the Director, are you going to face him down with your theory? How will you do that without involving the RCUP?"

"Good questions and as usual, good thinking, Frau. My current answers are I don't know. We'll just have to let events unfold further. I just wanted to be on the record with all of you and encouraging you to think along those lines. But let's not get ahead of ourselves."

(The one who seemed to be ahead of himself was the Great Bear but I had already made that point and wasn't about to do it again. At least, not now.)

"OK, we have a recital to attend. Thanks, Howard. Keep in touch."

Chapter Thirty Three

4 PM Saturday – Winnipeg Opera

Lots of jitters and possibly fright
Leading up to an opening night.
When it's time to go on
All the nerves will be gone.
The recital will turn out just right.

Emotions and noise levels both rose to a crescendo as the final hours leading to an eight o'clock curtain flickered across the auditorium count-down clock. At the moment, the singers, accompanied by Bearyl, were down in the costume room going through the agonies of last minute fittings and adjustments. Even Lepi, who had eschewed theatrical attire in Scotland *(his pelt and luxurious tail was really all he needed.)* succumbed to wearing an abbreviated Unmountie Red Serge jacket for one number and a lumberjack shirt and axe for another. Bearnice had four changes of dress ranging from glitter and glitz to Indian Buckskin.

Onstage and backstage, the TV crew was testing out the cameras, mikes, cables and shot lists. Stagehands and lighting techs were shouting to each other and moving ladders and dollies around the proscenium. Members of the orchestra were dribbling in as the Music Director and Orchestra Leader went through yet another round of artistic decisions. The sound of vacuum cleaners echoed across the hall, making conversations difficult and sporadic. In short, peace and quiet were long lost commodities.

Our team was scattered around the Center. At the moment, Otto was back in the Director's office looking for any additional "clues." He seemed to be really into this "detective stuff." The Frau and Colonel had taken up their protective roles down at the wardrobe rooms. L. Condor was up in the balcony, watching the proceedings and occasionally spreading his wings. At the Edinbeargh Opera, those wings came in very handy in foiling the attempted murder of the Bearoness. *(Book Three – The Case of Scotch)* Madame Catherine and her photographer were chatting up various and sundry crew and orchestra members for some background and local color. Octavius and I were sitting in his specially adapted box seats.

"There are still too many loose ends in this situation," he rumbled.

"Too many? That's all there are. Everything seems to point to the Director but the "whys" just won't come into focus. This thing seems to stretch back years and there's more we need to know about his time in Germany and England. His on-again, off-again relationship with Honoria is puzzling. They seemed to be working together but who knows. And what the hell was Felicia Foxx up to? That cutie had an agenda all her own. Why did she make those trips to Munich and Manchester long after the wolverine and cow had skipped town? Digging up dirt? Creating blackmail scenarios? Where was her money coming from? No administrative assistant I know of could afford her lifestyle."

"Have we heard anything further from Shetland Yard?"

"No, I think Superintendent Wardlaw is giving all his information to the RCUP before he talks with us. He's an interesting guy. None of this has any effect on his patch but he's dedicated a lot of time and resources to it."

"I think he's bored." said the Bear. "Lucky for us. He's a really good cop. A bit stiff but smart, energetic and resourceful."

"By the way, shouldn't we be hearing from our Canadian friends in law enforcement? I know it's a Saturday but the RCUP doesn't seem to watch clocks or calendars."

"I'm expecting a call from Rowan. If not, I think he's coming to tonight's recital. You did provide him with tickets, didn't you?"

"Center section, ten rows back. The acoustic sweet spot. We all have tickets in that area, except for you, of course, and Condo. He wanted a front row seat in the balcony. I think he sees it as a launch point. I also got tickets for Forrest Fox and his mate as well as Kitty and Maxie from Kitty's Kozy Korner. They're the bar owners that confirmed the kids' story. You haven't met them, have you? Opera lovers and a real sketch."

The Bear's phone rang. "Bear here!" he shouted, startling several of the cleaning crew who immediately resumed their vacuuming and picking up. "What's that Rowan? Sorry, this place is a bedlam. I'm having trouble hearing you. Tell you what. Can you meet me at the hotel at six? We can have a drink and come back over to the center together. OK?"

"Maury, get a hold of the Colonel. We need him to drive us back to the Ratison."

*****

5:45 PM – Ratison Hotel Lobby Bar

"I think he said he had big news. I should have called him back from outside the center, but this way we can all get in on the discussion." said the Bear.

The Colonel, Octavius and I were waiting for Superintendent Caballus to make an appearance while nursing our favorite libations. My cell phone rang. Otto!

"Hi Otto. What's shakin'?"

"Not me, Maury. The Director is nowhere to be found *(no big surprise there.)* I've gone over his office with the proverbial fine tooth comb and came up with a couple of strange things. There are several memo pads and pens with a German logo on them. What does "Starke Musik" mean?"

"I don't know. Let me put Octavius on."

"Hello Otto! Yes, I speak German. *(among thirty two other languages)* It could mean several things but the most likely is "Strong Music" or "Music of Power." You found the logo on some pads and pens? Careless of him to leave them behind. Probably from the agency he was running in Munich. See if you can find anything on the Internet, and I'll call Superintendent Wardlaw. He can take it up with Interpol. There may be nothing we don't already know, but it's worth a follow-up. Anything else?"

"Yeah, I was checking out his executive bathroom when one of the cleaning staff walked in. I zapped out, but I'm not sure whether I was seen or not. I didn't see her rushing out in a panic or calling anyone, so I probably got away with it. There were several bandages and some hydrogen peroxide in the medicine cabinet. The bottle was half empty and the bandage package had been opened."

"Sounds like he has a wound of some sort, doesn't it? Did you find anything in the safe?"

"Nope! Absolutely empty. Have the RCUP been able to re-assemble any of the shredded items?"

"I don't know. We're waiting right now for Superintendent Caballus. In fact, here he comes. We'll be back at the center about seven. We can talk further then."

He hung up and greeted the police horse who was decked out in a very stylish semi-formal blanket. "Good evening, Rowan. Is your mate with you?"

"No, she's meeting me at the recital. Thanks again for the tickets. She loves vocal music. Sings a bit herself, in fact."

"Delighted. Now that the noise level is acceptable and *(looking around)* we seem to be away from any curiosity seekers, let's hear your news. You remember Maury and the Colonel, of course."

"Yes, I do! *(nod of the head)* Gentlebeasts! Well, we're going to have a bit of re-thinking to do. Ottawa came back with an analysis of the hairs taken from the cow's wounds. They're not wolverine. They're from a bear – black, brown or grizzly. You may be a suspect, Octavius!"

They both laughed *(whinnied and roared)* startling the lobby staff and the patrons.

"Well," I said. "That puts Grigor Gregory back on the prime probable perp list, doesn't it?"

"It certainly does. I intend to hold him for questioning. Several of my animals are on their way to the center now."

"Wait a second, Rowan. Let's do a little strategizing here. He's responsible for televising the recital tonight. If it's not him, *(a long shot, I'll admit)* you'll have turned the event into a circus. I'm sure we can keep him under surveillance and hemmed in until the taping is over. Then we can quietly take him into custody. His attorney, Forrest Fox, will be in the audience. We'll inform him after the show."

"I'm not sure of this, Octavius. I'd hate to tell my superiors that a murder suspect escaped because we didn't want to disturb a musical recital."

"Between your staff and mine, I'm sure we can keep it contained. Besides, there are still a number of questions we need to unravel about the Opera Director. He's in the mix somewhere. Let's not scare him off. And there's still Felicia Foxx to consider."

"OK, but I don't know how long it would take to skin a Horse and Kodiak Bear alive, but I'm sure the Commissioner would be delighted to take on the task, if we blow this. I'll call the team and tell them to stay at the center, but hang back. If anyone asks, we can say that we have taken police precautions at the recital because of the murders."

I piped up, "Have your experts gotten anything out of the shredder contents from the Director's office?"

"They've been able to reassemble quite a few documents. We're trying to analyze them now."

"By the way, Rowan," said the Bear, "do you know anything about a German outfit called *Starke Musik* – Strong Music? Seems the Director had ties to it in some way."

"Not familiar to me, but that's what we have electronics for. I'll check."

"So will we." said the Bear.

The Development of Civilization Volume 4 Part 3
Music and Dance
(From "An Introduction to Faunapology" by Octavius Bear Ph.D.)

Among the many characteristics that separated Homo Sapiens from the other animals on Pre-Big Shock Earth, none was more fascinating than their abilities to sing, dance and respond to rhythms. It was much later as linguistic development progressed that H.Saps developed the ability to speak in rhyme and thus combine meaningful messages in measured cadences and sweeping vocal arrangements – in other words, songs with lyrics.

To be sure, many other animals were quite capable of creating noises that could often be quite intricate and significant, often approaching the sophistication of song as we know it. Mating dances were and still are quite common among many species although most lacked repetitive and complex rhythms such as we have today.

When the Big Shock hit, essentially wiping out H.Saps and whatever civilizing advances they had made, this might also have been the end of any further progression of music and dance on earth. Fortunately, among the many skills induced in the remaining species by the sudden and spectacular enhancement of their nervous systems and brain functions, the basic elements of musical development were among those improved and disseminated. Primitive dances to celebrate victory, declare war, seek a mate or express joy or sorrow blossomed slowly but deliberately into art forms for their own sake. Similarly, singing took on a wide spectrum of emotional significance. Other purposes for both song and dance evolve, not the least of which was sheer entertainment and enjoyment of beauty. This created the seeds of artistic appreciation which to this day is by no means universal or consistent around the world. My masterpiece may be your noise!

Initially the beauty of song depended in large part on the voices of the singers. But soon, the budding tool-making skills of the post Big Shock fauna were also devoted to further enhancing sounds and then music. The first musical instruments may have been accidents or simply attempts to amplify sound. From this however, followed the discovery, amazing in retrospect, that devices could be made that would not only replicate but extend well beyond the range, timbre and volume of the animal voice. By combining these devices, in the paws and claws of skilled practitioners, the first primitive orchestras came to light.

Few pre-Big Shock species had a sense of complex rhythm. H.Sap. could produce drumming sounds by beating on hollow gourds or logs but these were often simply repetitive drones. The perception of cadence and the ability to create it seems to be at least partly the result of imitative behavior – group dancing, another facility enhanced in most species after the Big Shock. Reproducing a beat and overlaying complex rhythmic formations represent another major stage in our musical progress.

All told, our progression to such sophisticated and varied musical and dance forms ranging from opera to rock and ballet to the Carnaval Samba gives some hope that we will not again regress to our more barbaric stages even though many other backward signs suggest that we have not travelled all that far since the Big Shock.

Welcome to The Winnipeg Opera
The Canadian Debut Recital of

Ms. Bearnice Blanc and Mr. 猫 Leperello

Orchestra under the Direction of Hartley Hare
<u>PROGRAMME</u>

Duet: O Canada *by Lavallée and Weir*

Solo: Elise's Fur *by Ludwig von Bearthoven*

Duet: Indian Love Howl *by Wolfgang Frizzle*

Solo: Drinking Song from the Tails of Beijing *by 猫 Leperello*

Duet: Lacrymosa from Requiem *by Hector Bearlioz*

Interval

Duet: Selections from "Kits" *by Andrew Laird Webear*

Solo: Love Songs from the Motion Picture *7.63* *by Federico Feline*

Solo: Stouthearted Cats *by Siegfried Rombearg*

Duet: Death Scene from Romeo and Juliet *by Charles Gooneybird*

Duet: The Lumberjack Song *by M.Python* with the RCUP Choristers

Duet: Bonnie Annie Laurie *Traditional*

The Winnipeg Opera extends its

sincere thanks to the following benefactors who

made this evening's performance possible:

The Flora and Fauna Futures Fund

The Bruin Foundation

Universal Ursine Industries

Friends of the Winnipeg Opera

This concert is being televised for future broadcast. Only pre-authorized, professional photographers may take pictures during the performance.

Please turn off all cell phones and pagers during the concert

The Artists are represented by the Meerkat Global Talent Agency

Chapter Thirty Four

7 PM Saturday – Winnipeg Opera

Yes, the moment is practically here
It's the biggest event of the year.
When our singers are done
We'll all join in the fun!
Just get ready to stand up and cheer.

The long wait was almost over. The doors to the center's lobby swung open. Kiosks hawking Opera recordings; wine bars offering bowls of not too great vintages; modest snacks on display; lines building up for the rest rooms; tickets being picked up at the box office. Time for another concert!

But not just another concert. The murder of Honoria Heifer had cast a grotesque shadow on the proceedings. Morbid curiosity merged with musical interest.

"Just how good are these two? They were a big hit in Scotland. But what do the Scots know about music? North American tastes are totally different. Do you think there'll be another murder? Thank goodness there's no chandelier for the Phantom to drop. I hear both of them are real lookers. Even if they can't sing, they can always pose. Let's get our programmes and seats."

And so it went. Backstage, last minute panics rose and swiftly fell. Check and recheck. For a stage crew used to mounting major operas, this was a walk in the park. Two performers, center stage; basic light cues; raising and lowering a couple of scrims; but the TV cameras, mikes and lights were a different story. Otto watched as Grigor Gregory, headset askew with annotated

223

musical scores in his paws, went over some final notes with the conductor. If anyone wondered about the police presence in the wings, they just wrote it off as protective overkill. *(bad metaphor).*

In the pit, the sounds of tuning instruments grated on a few nerves.

The singers had just returned from doing an interview in the Green Room with Beatrice Beaver of CWP-TV. No mention of the murders or how close the two of them had come to being arrested and charged with the crime. No mention of Felicia Foxx's demise, either. Just a gushing *(and lisping)* review of the evening's program, their professional backgrounds and future plans. In short, an agent's dream!

Now, in the dressing rooms, Bearyl and the Frau were calming Bearnice down. "Look at it this way" her twin said. "At least, you don't have Honoria giving you agita."

In Lepi's room, I was acting as agent to the stars. "Packed house, kiddo! You're gonna flatten their fur. Do I smell huge concert tours? Get ready for the big time. You might want to run a comb through your tail again."

The Colonel had posted himself outside the auditorium in case Opera Director Wolverine decided to show his face. Usually, he made the opening remarks before the concerts began. Tonight, Herr Professor Doktor Dieter von Tripp, the Musical Director would be doing the honors.

Octavius had taken his place in his modified box seat and was chatting briefly with Superintendent Caballus, once again well turned out in a formal blanket. His mate was also standing there, chatting with Condo who had

224

stopped by before taking his place in the balcony. She gave out a couple of demure horse laughs as the condor changed voices on her several times.

As the warning chimes rang out calling everyone to their seats, Forrest Fox and his mate made a last minute dash down the aisle. Once seated, he looked over at Octavius who mouthed, "Let's meet at the intermission. Important!"

Our team took up our assigned positions, except, of course for Otto who would be zapping back and forth to the Director's office and the backstage outer doors. I joined Octavius and was amazed to see Chita sitting next to him on the other side. I'm sure Octavius was delighted. Cheetah chutzpah! *(Yes, Yes, I know!)* She looked over and winked at me. Her photographer was one of the authorized professionals allowed to roam the house.

The house lights dimmed, and to a smattering of applause, the Musical Director stepped out from behind the curtain, briefly catching his antlers as he emerged. Small titters of laughter.

"Good evening, dear friends. I am Doktor Dieter von Tripp, Musical Director of the Winnipeg Opera. It is my great pleasure to welcome you to this, the first Canadian recital of two new musical talents whose voices, I am sure, will enthrall you. We believe that they are well on their way to stardom, and we are thrilled to assist them on their journey. I speak of course, of Manitoba's own Bearnice Blanc and her partner Mr. Leperello. Please give them a traditional *Winnipeg Welcome* as Maestro Hartley Hare strikes up the first notes of our national anthem."

And so he did and they did. The curtains swept aside, to a thunderous burst of applause, leaving the stars of the evening bathed in spotlights in front of a very large Canadian flag. Bearnice and Lepi sang the first verse of *O Canada* alone and then encouraged the audience to sing the remaining verses with them. You can well imagine *(or maybe you can't)* the mixture of sounds emerging from the mouths of several hundred different species – including the roar of a nine foot tall Kodiak bear. I once remember Octavius drowning out a massive crowd of baseball enthusiasts as they sang *The Star Spangled Banner* during the World Series.

The concert was off to a very promising start. As the first part of the programme moved on, Rowan Caballus and Octavius *(me actually)* kept a check on Grigor's whereabouts and any possible stirrings at or near the Director's office. Unbeknownst to us, Chita had clued in her photographer, as he pointed his lenses hither and yon, to keep an eye out for the wolverine. One false alarm on that score. There was indeed, a wolverine couple in the audience.

This raised an interesting issue. Our team had met the Director and knew what he looked like. Dark brown with an off-white face mask and body stripes. Quite distinctive! The police, on the other hand, may or may not have a clear idea of his appearance. Not too much of a problem this evening, with all their concentration focused on the grizzly bear but wolverine colorations and facial characteristics varied significantly. Note to self: Get a hold of the Associate Director and get some publicity photos of Doctor Woodrow *(Werner?)* Wolverine. The police may have some already but what the hell!

The first half of the programme ended with a passionate rendering of the Lacrymosa from Bearlioz' Requiem. Standing Ovation! Two for two! First Edinbeargh, and now Winnipeg. Agent Maury had himself a pair of winners.

After a prolonged series of bows, Bearnice and Lepi ran backstage to their dressing rooms. Costume changes for Part Two. Once again the Frau and Bearyl set to in helping Bearnice while I stood idly by in Lepi's dressing room. He was going on sans attire until he had to make a quick offstage change for the Lumberjack Song. Plaid shirt and oversize axe. Bearnice appeared midway through the song as a sweet young Canadian maiden along with a chorus of red clad RCUP constables.

On stage and backstage many eyes were tracking the movements of Grigor Gregory, primary candidate for Honoria Heifer's Homicide.

Chapter Thirty Five

9 PM Saturday – Winnipeg Opera

As the evening winds down to a close,
Is it safe for us all to suppose
Everything's simply great?
There's no room for debate?
It's too early for me to disclose.

Interval *(or if you prefer, intermission).* Forrest Fox had made his way over to Octavius' box, and listened as the Great Bear outlined the case against Grigor. He told the fox that as soon as the last curtain fell *(or earlier, if the grizzly tried to escape)* the police were going to take him into custody. Obviously, Forrest wanted to be with his client. Octavius promised one of our team would see the fox's mate home from the concert. Shaking his head, the lawyer returned to his seat and entered into a brief conversation with his companion. She looked over at Octavius, who nodded and extended his paws in her direction. She nodded back, none too graciously. However, that's part of the cost of being a high priced attorney's wife. It goes with the house and clothes.

I had returned to the ursine box just as Forrest was leaving. Madame Catherine was not in her seat and then I spotted her in the back talking with her photographer. When she returned Octavius said, "Look, you probably know we are planning to arrest Grigor Gregory as soon as the show is over. NO CLOSE-UP PICTURES!! Keep your photographer a safe distance away from the event. Back stage will be a chaotic mess to begin with. We don't want to create more chaos or give him a chance to escape"

"We still have to determine what, if any, role the Opera Director played in the murders. We have yet to figure out how Felicia Foxx fits into this thing. There are too many open switches in this case to suit me."

Chita nodded her head but said nothing. That could have meant anything.

The house lights started to dim. Conversations dropped off. Last minute returnees hurried to their seats causing the usual amount of upset. "Scuse me, scuse me, sorry, Oh was that your paw? No, don't get up! Well, I never!"

Part two of the recital was about to begin.

*****

The second half was moving along superbly. The audience had already decided that here indeed was a musical phenomenon and was showing its wild appreciation. The entire auditorium joined in singing "He's a lumberjack and he's OK" and then broke out in uproarious laughter as the song collapsed under its own silliness. Bearnice played the part of the shocked and disappointed maiden in full Academy Award style and then tearfully rushed off the stage. *(For her next and last costume change.)* Lepi marched off with the "Unmountie Chorus."

Back for their final number, *Annie Laurie*, leaving tear-filled eyes throughout the house! Standing ovation! Pounding on the seats! "Brava, Bravo, Encore, Encore!"

As the two vocalists sang their way further into Manitoba's memories, the RCUP minions were positioning themselves back stage to surround Grigor Gregory. Forrest Fox had gotten up during one of the standing ovations and headed for the entrance to the wings. So did the Colonel and Frau. Both of them covered their actions by tossing bouquets at the smiling artists. Somehow the condor had escaped notice and had set himself up on one of the floodlight arrays above the stage. Madame Catherine had disappeared and I stayed with Octavius as he trundled down one of the side aisles. Otto was still shifting back and forth from the Director's office to the backstage entry to the executive wing. Woodrow Wolverine was still a no-show.

The curtain fell for the last time. The two performers rushed off the stage and the RCUP rushed to surround Grigor Gregory. Amid the noises from the auditorium and the to-and-from rushing on stage, an equine shout could still be heard. "Grigor Gregory. This is the Royal Canadian Unmounted Police. You are under arrest for the murder of Honoria Heifer." The Grizzly dropped the head set he had been wearing, looked around, saw that his exit paths were blocked by the police, stage hands and other players including us. He looked over at his on-again lawyer who nodded in return. He then held out his paws to be cuffed. Forrest Fox said, "I am the legal representative of Mr. Gregory and will accompany him as you take him into custody. We will have no statement until my client and I have had time to confer." Surrounded by members of the police, they were rushed out of the stage entrance into a waiting van.

Octavius and I had arrived on the scene just in time to see Grigor Gregory taken away with Forrest Fox. He looked around for the Colonel. "Wyatt, let's you, the Frau, Maury and I get down to RCUP headquarters right now. We can leave Otto and Condo here in case the Director makes a surprise visit."

Out in the Green Room, Lepi and Bearnice, were lapping up champagne along with the kudos of the audience members, Bearyl, Opera staff *(minus the Director),* Chita and her photographer, Kitty and Maxie, Forrest Fox's wife and the news team from CWP-TV. Beatrice Beaver had a microphone in paw and cameraman at the ready, little knowing that she was missing out on covering the arrest of the TV station's producer on a charge of murder.

Condo made a short visit and then relieved Otto so he could get his share of ursine hugs from a giggling, tearful Bearnice. Lepi was busy posing with a variety of obviously starry-eyed female admirers. All in all, an exciting evening.

Chapter Thirty Six

Midnight Saturday – RCUP Headquarters

Well, the Grizzly is under arrest
And we're trying to tell him it's best
In this desperate scene,
If he really comes clean.
It's the time that he simply confessed.

Charges read, paw prints and mug shots taken, possessions turned over and logged in the property room, rights read to the assumed assailant and a conference room set up for lawyer and client discussion.

Forrest looked at Grigor and said, "You realize that you are under arrest on suspicion of killing Honoria Heifer. While the police would also like to charge you with Felicia Foxx's death, their case, such as it is, doesn't hold much water yet. The major evidence against you in the cow's death is traces of bear blood and hair found on her body. They will be doing a DNA test to determine if those hairs are yours. They have already determined by testing that they came from a bear, probably a grizzly."

"Felicia was strangled but there is nothing in the evidence to directly tie you to her death, although the circumstances seem pretty coincidental. Your co-worker, Charlie seems able to provide you with a time alibi on that one. For the moment, I recommend you say nothing to the police on advice of counsel. Let them establish their trail of evidence."

"As soon as the courts open, I will be entering a plea for bail. Given the nature of the crime, that won't be easy but Octavius Bear has promised to provide the money if we can't get a bail bondsman to commit. He's here with his team and they want to talk with you in private. I don't like the idea but since anything you say to them can't be entered as evidence and he's footing the bill for my services, I guess I'll go along with it. Superintendent Caballus has agreed, somewhat reluctantly. Are you willing to see him?"

"Why not? But I won't tell him anything. If he wants to kill his time, that's up to him. I suppose I should be grateful to him for putting up the money and employing you but not grateful enough to confess to the cow's murder."

"I wouldn't expect you to. In fact, I'm not quite sure why he wants to talk with you. He has a couple of members of his team with him. You can back out or stop the conversation anytime you want."

"OK, send them in."

Forrest came out of the room and waved at us. Octavius turned to the colonel and asked, "Can you tell if the police have surveillance devices active in that room?"

"Not for certain but I wouldn't be surprised. It's a shame we don't have Condo with us. He could pick them off immediately. Let us try."

The two wolves entered the room, waved at Grigor and gave him a "don't talk" signal. They gave the room a quick scan and called out to Octavius, "Let's ask for a change in venue and tell Forrest he's been spied on."

Amid protests to the contrary, the police reluctantly agreed to change rooms. Caballus promised there was no surveillance in a van owned by the local hospital and parked in the RCUP garage. With two guards stationed outside, the group squeezed *(Octavius!)* into the vehicle.

"OK, Doctor Bear, I'm here. Thanks for agreeing to fund my cause. Now what do you want to know?"

"No, It's what we want you to know!"

(Thus began a major bluff on Octavius' part based 99% on his sniff test.)

"Look, Grigor, we know you're not from here!"

"Sure, no news there. I'm originally from the States."

"No. you're not. Oh, you may have started in the States when you arrived here from *(We call it Gaea. I don't know what you call it.)*"

The grizzly looked thunderstruck. "I don't know what you're talking about!"

"Of course you do, and we believe that Honoria and the Director of the Opera are also Gaeans or whatever you call yourselves. Felicia Foxx may have been one, too."

"Are you crazy?"

"No, just informed! Now, let's stop playing games. We're not trying to get you convicted. We're concerned about a whole different issue. Different worlds where Homo Sapiens still survives and lives in cooperation with intelligent animals like yourself. We call it the Multiverse Phenomenon. What's your name for it?"

(Envision if you will, a nine foot, 1400 pound Kodiak way out on a flimsy theoretical limb trying to exude confidence, nay even arrogance, in expounding his Alternative Universe theory. The next crash you hear…)

"You are crazy!"

"Not quite," said the colonel, "we've been to your world or one damn close to it and we're concerned. What are you doing here? How did you get here? What do you want?"

"I want to get out of this van. Hey, guard!"

"Listen first," said the Frau, "and then we'll step aside and let you go stew in your own murderous juice. If you want our help, we need to hear from you. Now!"

(Nothing like two authoritative wolves backing up a formidable bear to make one alter one's viewpoint.)

My turn, "We have serious scientific reason to believe that a wide range of quantum super-positioned worlds exist in this cosmos. *(Yes, this is me talking!)* We also have reason to believe that in these worlds over 100,000 years ago an incredible solar blast took place, altering the nature of the species in existence at the time."

"Homo Sapiens was a pivotal figure. In some worlds like this one, they died out and other highly developed animal species survived. In others, nobody truly intelligent is at home at all. Then there's your world. We think both Homo Sapiens survived and Advanced Animals evolved. And we think you and a few other animals like the Director and possibly Honoria and Felicia are here on some kind of spy mission or possibly you're fugitives from your own world or…"

Octavius picked up on it. "If the Homo Sapiens in your world came here, it would only be a matter of time before they were discovered in our all-animal world. However, your kind would and has been able to blend in rather smoothly. You look, sound and act like us, in large part. I'll reserve judgment on the cow. How are we doing in the theory department? Think about this. We have no interest in blowing the whistle and setting off a worldwide panic unless you guys are a real threat. If that's the case then a murder rap is only the beginning for you. If you're here for benign reasons, we need to know. Killing a cow, albeit a very annoying cow, hardly speaks to kindly intent. Now, if you want our help, you have to level with us. You'll have to trust us but then we'll have to trust you, too."

The grizzly blew out his cheeks, looked up at the ceiling of the van and then shook his head affirmatively. "OK, you're partially right. We are from a different world. Oddly enough, we call it Earth. Ironic, huh? And you have the quantum mechanics scheme right for the most part. We've been here for about ten years now. There's a very small number of us. Less than fifty, I'd guess. Very few of our animal species can make the transit and Homo Sapiens can't do it at all. Like many of these things, we discovered it by accident. We had been individually travelling to other worlds and it was only when we came in contact with each other in a different world, not yours, that we realized there were a number of us. We've been spending most of our time tracking down our own adepts. This is an especially good place to operate from because, as you say, we blend right in. We stay in smaller cities to avoid unnecessary exposure, at least for moment."

"Like Munich and Manchester and Winnipeg? Why can't you do it from your home world?"

"The Homo Sapiens who know about us are trying to eliminate us. They're afraid we'll use our abilities to take over our own Earth by attacking from other worlds. Crazy, of course. There's only a few of us and none of us know how to control our talent. With one or two exceptions. The Director is one of the more 'talented' ones. He can travel at will. I'm a passive. I need to be transported but once at my destination, I function completely. Honoria also was a 'talent' but she got out of hand. She started challenging the Director. She had planned to use these recitals to publicly tell your world about us and make an attempt at assuming total leadership. She was too dangerous to allow her to go on. We stopped her."

Dead silence! Then the Colonel asked. "What about Felicia Foxx?"

"Felicia is, was, from your world but she began to pick up inklings of who we were while she worked in the Director's office. After she quit the Opera and came to CWP, she had access to all kinds of news stories that seemed innocuous to most of you but very meaningful to us. It was a way for us to keep track of one another. That was why I was assigned to CWP. Direct news links around the world."

"What were you going to do with all this information?" I asked.

"I don't know. The Director doesn't share much but I'm sure he's concocting plans and carefully making contacts among your influentials. He's not a very nice animal."

"I guess Felicia felt safe working at the station but then she got more and more curious and greedy. After she returned from a few trips to Germany and England, she faced down the Director with what she had found out. She wanted pay for her silence. She also offered to work for us. She was the one who trapped Honoria. But I guess that sealed her fate. I had nothing to do with her death. I'm sure you can guess who did."

Octavius simply nodded. "Well, I think that ties things up for the moment. This story stays with us. You can tell your lawyer whatever you want but I'd follow his guidance on talking to the police. I'll see whether you're going to need bail on Monday. Guard! We're finished here. You can take Mr. Gregory back to his cell. We'll be in touch."

Outside the RCUP offices, I yawned and said to the Great Bear, "Knowing what we now know about him, are you still going to try to bail him out?"

"I don't think we'll have the chance," he replied.

Chapter Thirty Seven

Midday Sunday – Winnipeg Opera

Now what will the wolverine do
When the Sunday recitals are through?
Is the money a key?
Doesn't seem so to me!
Will he pull off a swift switcheroo?

Otto and Condo had taken turns watching the Director's office through the night. The cashier had taken the night's receipts from the box office and deposited them in the wolverine's safe. No other action. Events were slowly spinning back up for the three o'clock performance. The arrest of Grigor Gregory was now common knowledge. Wally Wapiti had chosen not to run the story on the morning TV news much to the chagrin of Beatrice Beaver and Morley Moose but he did assign Charlie as the replacement for taping the two remaining recitals.

The singers and Bearyl had managed to get some sleep after the impromptu partying in the Green Room. On our return to the hotel, Octavius had fallen off, whether naturally or narcoleptically, I can't tell. The wolves and I had returned to our rooms for some curtailed shut eye. Nobody knew where Madame Catherine had disappeared to. Probably taking a cat nap. Otto and Condo had sacked out, spelling each other at the Center.

Now the team, minus Bearnice, Lepi and Bearyl, had reassembled in the rehearsal room at the Opera Center. Chita had joined us and Octavius didn't seem to mind. Strange! Discussion on what we had learned and what we should tell Forrest and the RCUP. We decided to tell both of them that we had even stronger reasons to believe the Director was the true perp of both murders but in the interest of not scaring him off, we were keeping the rest of the story at bare bones status. I'm sure we'll get plenty of push back from Superintendent Caballus on that one. Forrest was getting together with his client and would get whatever information Grigor chose to give him.

Opinions were sharply divided on whether the Wolverine would make an appearance. If he was anywhere in the area, he probably knew about Grigor's arrest. It had been covered by radio, a competing TV station and the morning newspapers. What he probably didn't know was that his cover as a member of this world's fauna had been blown and that we were aware of his "active adept" status. We really didn't know what that meant. Could he literally appear and disappear at will? Did he have to be asleep in order to transit? Was he constrained to remain in this world? What did Grigor mean when he identified himself as a "passive."

Several of us were of the opinion that greed (or need) would overcome sense and that he would return after the last concert to remove the weekend proceeds from his safe. In any event, the RCUP would be back at each performance. And so would we!

*****

240

For a while, the afternoon degenerated into full scale disorder. Bearnice developed a serious case of *'second performance jitters'*, the singers' equivalent of the sophomore jinx, and Bearyl, Chita and the Frau set about calming her down. Lepi was his usual stoic self. Opera management kept upsetting the production staffs by sticking their snouts into the various preparations but no sign of Director Wolverine. Wally Wapiti was on hand to oversee Charlie's performance as TV producer. Actually, he told us, the first recordings went so well that the next tapings were just safety standbys or possible pickups of an unusual event or two. He kept shaking his antlered head about Grigor.

Octavius, Forrest Fox and Superintendent Caballus were down in the rehearsal room bringing their collective wisdom to bear *(!)* on how to deal with the missing wolverine. The RCUP's dragnet had come up with nothing thus far.

During the morning, Grigor had given the police a heavily redacted version of what he had told us. He confessed to assisting Woodrow Wolverine in killing off Honoria Heifer but said nothing about motive or background. He did implicate Felicia Foxx in the cow's killing but denied having anything to do with her own death. Most of all, he said not a word about coming from an alternate universe with Honoria and the Director. As far as the RCUP was concerned, these were nasty but unexceptional murders.

Once again, the question arose. How much did the Wolverine know? If he was aware of Grigor's confession, would he just fade away into the sunset or make a desperate pass at the money and other contents of his office before disappearing?

The afternoon's recital was a howling success. *(Sorry!)* Wildly favorable reviews from the Saturday night performance had helped fill the Sunday afternoon seats and created a land rush for evening tickets. Truly, the Bear-Cat as they were now being called, were an overnight sensation. Kitty and Maxie had organized a Bear-Cat Happy Hour for all of their patrons who had testified to Bearnice's and Lepi's innocence. *(Sergeant Preston was not invited.)*

Manitoba media were slobbering over themselves to interview them. They were already booked into Toronto for two evenings and then they would cross the border for a five state tour in the American Midwest. Agent Maury on the job!

But as the evening approached, still no sign of the Director.

Frau Schuylkill joined the three legal strategists in the rehearsal room. "Gentlebeasts, may I offer a suggestion?"

"Of course," said the Bear, "your ideas are always welcome."

"This evening, after the first act, the box office will be closed. I could suggest that the cashier might want to get home a bit earlier to spend what is left of the evening with her family. There wasn't supposed to be a performance tonight. I could accompany her up to the Director's office during intermission and wait while she deposits the evening's proceeds in his safe along with the monies from the other two performances. If the Director is hiding in the executive area, he may want to use the cover of the second act to get in and get out. We can keep Otto in the lavatory and the colonel, Senhor Condor and I can keep watch. It may amount to nothing but it would be his best opportunity to take advantage of the distractions on the stage and the surrounding area."

"Well, we haven't come up with any better plan and it might just work. What do you think, Rowan?"

"It sounds good to me. I have my men stationed around backstage and if he's here at all, he'll want to avoid them. Let's try it."

Chapter Thirty Eight

Sunday Nine PM – Winnipeg Opera

The recital has gone simply grand.
The Director is taken in hand.
Is there anything more
That we're holding in store?
It's a mystery, you understand!

The Bear-Cat singers had just launched into the tearful Lacrymosa from Bearlioz' Requiem that would conclude the first act. The cashier had organized the evening's receipts into bags ready for pickup by the Armored Car service in the morning. Frau Schuylkill and Colonel Where waited while, totally unaware of what was really going on, she locked the bags, shut the box office door and joined them in the passageway to the executive stairs. They were carrying small pistols hidden in their formal clothing. *(Next stop: Green Room Party and then a more opulent event back at the Ratison.)* Otto had zapped into the Director's washroom, ready to create *"alarums and excursions."* Octavius, Chita and I were in our seats near the back of the auditorium, with quick access to the executive stairs, dividing our attention between the music and the possible general turmoil. *(No, not him!)* Once again, Condo had secured a seat on a light bar and was sweeping the hall with his high resolution eyes. The police concentrated on the exits and backstage. Caballus and his mate were rigged out in formal get-up and acting like they were enjoying a major social event. Waves here, smiles there, occasional laughs!

The cashier entered the Director's office as the last few notes dissolved into thundering applause. She unlocked the safe, added the bags to its contents, closed the door, spun a few dials, walked back out into the hall, thanked the waiting wolves and headed off for wherever. Now, was anything going to happen? One or two of the Opera staff made short-cut transits down the executive hallway getting ready for the second half. Muted noises from the auditorium and lobby. Otto checked his phone connection with the wolves and the police. The Frau and Colonel took up station in the Associate Director's office next door. Down stairs, Octavius, Chita and I socialized and listened in on Otto's connection upstairs. Nothing!

*****

And as they say over and over in the theatre, *the houselights dimmed* and most, but not all of the audience returned to their seats. Guess who were out of their places and on the alert? (*I know, you're trying to imagine Octavius, all 9 feet and 1400 pounds of him, trying to be unobtrusive. Well, the lights were down; all attention was on the stage and the orchestra; the curtain was rising; and Octavius was standing next to a full size statue of the Center's major benefactor, Horatio Moose. A National Geographic tableau.*)

Upstairs. One minute nothing, the next minute, the Wolverine was there and unlocking his door. The colonel warned Otto over the headset. "Careful, he's coming in."

As soon as he had the door opened, the wolves swarmed out of the Associate Director's office and hurled themselves at the Director. He squirmed loose, spotted Otto and grabbed him around the neck. "Back off, you fools, or this one gets a broken neck like the fox."

They backed away but the colonel whispered into Otto's headset. "Get ready to zap!"

"All right," said the Frau, "Get the money out of the safe and leave but let go of our friend."

The wolverine howled, "The money? Who wants the money? Those bags are full of credit and debit card receipts and checks. The cash wouldn't get me a cross-town taxi ride. No, I want something else. Something much more important!"

"Zap, Otto!!"

The Director suddenly found himself with arms full of air. The otter had disappeared. Shocked, he charged at the wolves and got past them out the door where he ran into a spotted whirlwind who tackled him and jumped on his back. The wolves, Chita and two police dogs who had arrived on the scene finally subdued him.

Pawcuffed fore and aft, they dragged him off amid howls of roaring wolverine laughter.

Down on the stage, the lumberjack and his stage RCUP companions were wrapping up their comedy routine with another type of laughter. Once again, CWP-TV had missed out on recording a major arrest.

In the back of the auditorium, listening in on his headset, Octavius smiled to himself. "Damned clever, these Gaeans."

Superintendent Caballus strode up and said, "Well, we have him."

"Yes, you have, Rowan, make sure you keep him."

The horse looked at him quizzically but then turned off to give instructions to the arresting officers.

I looked up at Octavius. "What did that mean?"

"I'll tell you later. This hasn't completely played out yet."

He was interrupted by waves of applause as the last notes of *Annie Laurie* died out on the stage.

Chapter Thirty Nine

2 AM Monday – Ratison Ballroom

Now, there's really no use to pretend.
You can see that we've come to the end.
Is our 'tail' really through?
Well, I leave it to you
Are we finished or not, my dear friend?

The triumphant revelry was still going on loudly and hilariously. Hugs and smooches, smooches and hugs. The Blanc twins giggled their ursine way through the "well dones" and "way-to-go's." *(Bearyl was also getting her fair share of attention from the well-wishers.)* Lepi, as usual, was stoic but seemed to be sliding into an Oriental trance. Kitty and Maxie were doing their best to keep the carousing going by drunkenly singing chorus after chorus of the Indian Love Howl.

I got a chance to announce the details of the upcoming Bear-Cat tour in Canada and Midwest USA to rounds of cheers and wild applause. I also mentioned Bearyl's new role as Lady Macbearth. More cheers. Octavius made a short speech of congratulations as did the Associate Director of the Opera. Both carefully avoided any mention of the arrests of the Director or of Grigor. Wally Wapiti, Beatrice and Morley all were slinging down champagne in true "members of the media" style. Beatrice Beaver was really ticked off at missing out on coverage of both arrests.

Our team, minus Octavius who was uncharacteristically schmoozing elsewhere, had gathered off on one side of the room and was engaged in trying to sort out the evening's non-musical events. The Frau seemed puzzled and somewhat disappointed that her theory about the money as incentive had proven wrong. But what was the incentive? Why had the Wolverine gone to his office? What was the "something much more important" that walked him into their waiting arms? For the hundredth time she checked to make sure that Otto had not suffered any damage in the brief brawl. The Colonel, Condo, Otto and I all came to the same conclusion. It was almost as if the Wolverine wanted to be captured and arrested. But why?

Chita, watching the progress of her photographer, came over to the group and nudged the Frau. "I told you we could work together." The Frau concurred with dignity, "So you did! Madame Catherine! So you did!"

Superintendent Caballus was standing to one side with his mate casting a minor pall on the festivities. No one seemed anxious to chat up the police. No one also seemed to notice when an RCUP constable furtively walked up to the horse and whispered in his ear. The Super's ears went up, his eyes widened and he gave out an involuntary "whinnie!" He strode rapidly out of the room, leaving his mate flat-hoofed, stopping momentarily to say something to Octavius. The Great Bear nodded and then after the horse had left, he smiled and trundled over to our little group.

"Well, it seems my prediction was right."

"What prediction? What was that all about with the Superintendent?"

"It seems our two murderers have disappeared!"

"Disappeared?"

"Gone! They are no longer in the tender care of the RCUP."

Spurred on by an overdose of alcohol and my recent demonstrations of independence, I looked up at Octavius and squeaked. "All right, stop being so damn smug. Our team had a nasty tussle with that Wolverine, trying to capture him, and now you announce that you predicted he would vanish and take Grigor with him. You might have shared that bit of wisdom with us."

"I wasn't sure. There are a number of things I still don't know."

"For instance?"

"I don't know where they are."

The Colonel looked up and grinned. "The penny just dropped, Octavius. They pulled a Multiverse getaway. They could be anywhere."

"I think you're right, Colonel."

"But why the big effort to get himself arrested? Why didn't he just do a bunk?"

"Because Grigor couldn't!"

"Huh!"

"Remember Grigor told us the Director was an active adept. He could change universes at will. Grigor was a passive. He needed some kind of assist, someone to 'beam him up' so to speak. The Director had to be in the same location with Grigor, possibly even in the same room or cell. Then they could both disappear together. That was the "something more important." They may be anywhere. This world. Their home universe. Someplace altogether different. Remember Grigor also said there were about fifty or so Gaeans in small groups around our Earth. They may have joined up with any one of them. Woodrow or Werner Wolverine seems to be a leader, if not the leader."

"What do you think has happened to Grigor? Is he dead or alive?"

"I don't think he did himself any good by telling us what he did. They decided to kill off Honoria for wanting to go public about their presence here on Earth. He blabbed to us but we kept that part of the story from the police. On the other hand, he was the wolverine's trusted assistant. He may be too valuable to cast off. I don't know."

"Well," I said, "There's one thing I do know."

"What's that?"

"You're not going to have come up with Grigor's bail."

Bearoness Belinda
Béarnaise Bruin
(nee Black)

Epilogue

Seven Months Later – Bearmoral Castle

And so, as The Lower Case slowly sank into the West, we bade farewell to frigid Winnipeg, traveled back to the Bear's Lair in Cincinnati for a short period of R&R and are now ensconced in the newly opened and equally frigid Polar Paradise, formerly known as Bearmoral Castle. The Bearoness, now the mother of twin cubs, Arabella and McTavish, had re-converted the castle into its former self, a theme park / hotel, and reserved parts of the massive building and properties for the extended family *(us)*, friends and associates. Just about all the ready, willing and able citizens of Dunst are employed in one way or the other at the new resort which is taking reservations for almost a year in advance.

Belinda had ordered a stage and auditorium to be built around the Olympic size swimming pool in the castle and the Aquabear Review – *Some Like It Cold* – is currently in rehearsal, including the one and only Otto the Magnificent. Otto has been given a full bill of health by the UUI medical staff but still retains his illusionist skills and talents. We're not sure why. The Bearoness is also establishing with Madame Catherine Catt, no less, a genetic institute to follow up on the experimentation that Imperius Drake carried out on Otto. Drs. Vark and Bingbang from UUI are cooperating with this venture.

Elsewhere in the talent department, Bearyl is a great hit in her role of Lady Macbearth and has signed a contract for a major motion picture. Lepi and Bearnice are a smash with an extensive concert tour, TV appearances and recordings. They will also be resident talent at the hotel. Needless to say, I, your humble servant and agent to the ursine and lutrine stars, am having a ball in my not quite full time role as theatrical agent. Octavius, once he recovers from the shock of his new role as *Pater Familias,* will no doubt redirect my efforts.

Right now, besides chasing two brown and white fur balls and being protective of their bearonial mother, he has concentrated his efforts on expanding Project Multiverse. Howard and Condo have teamed up to further pursue the program and are gradually opening up our findings to other concerned organizations *(excluding General Turmoil.)* We still don't know the whereabouts or fate of Grigor Gregory and Werner Wolverine. We may never know.

The wolves, who have just formally mated, are busy supporting Howard and Condo in the Multiverse Project and are also providing air shuttle service between Cincinnati and the Shetlands. Belinda, after settling into her roles of mother, hotelier, showbear, research director and bearonial presence has also managed to search out a crew to replace Bearyl and Bearnice and return to flying the Aquabear SST. Bears in the Air!

Madame Catherine Catt is starting up a new Spotted Band in London with Jake, the jaguar and a couple of other musical felines, a serval and a margay. This while she edits and publishes *Purr* and *Sow* magazines. And oh, yes, her oil well, *The Hot Spot,* is alive and flowing.

Marlin is back with the Prince of Whales with a production version of an underwater communicator / translator fresh from the labs of UUI.

So things couldn't be going better, could they?

Then there was last night's phone call from Inspector Bruce Wallaroo in Sydney. "Ocko, he's back. I just shoved one of those barking Black Quack eggs into the harbor after two of my staff almost went bonkers from the noise. That *Damn Duck Didn't Die*."

End of

The Lower Case

Volume Four

Of the Casebooks of Octavius Bear

Also from MX Publishing

MX Publishing is the world's largest specialist Sherlock Holmes publisher, with over a hundred titles and fifty authors creating the latest in Sherlock Holmes fiction and non-fiction.

From traditional short stories and novels to travel guides and quiz books, MX Publishing cater for all Holmes fans.

The collection includes leading titles such as *Benedict Cumberbatch In Transition* and *The Norwood Author* which won the 2011 Howlett Award (Sherlock Holmes Book of the Year).

MX Publishing also has one of the largest communities of Holmes fans on Facebook with regular contributions from dozens of authors.

www.mxpublishing.com

Also From MX Publishing

London, 1920: Boston-bred Enoch Hale, working as a reporter for the Central News Syndicate, arrives on the scene shortly after a music hall escape artist is found hanging from the ceiling in his dressing room. What at first appears to be a suicide turns out to be murder.

Also coming in 2014 the second in the Enoch Hale series –
'The Poisoned Penman'.

www.mxpublishing.com

Also from MX Publishing

"Phil Growick's, 'The Secret Journal of Dr Watson', is an adventure which takes place in the latter part of Holmes and Watson's lives. They are entrusted by HM Government (although not officially) and the King no less to undertake a rescue mission to save the Romanovs, Russia's Royal family from a grisly end at the hand of the Bolsheviks. There is a wealth of detail in the story but not so much as would detract us from the enjoyment of the story. Espionage, counter-espionage, the ace of spies himself, double-agents, double-crossers...all these flit across the pages in a realistic and exciting way. All the characters are extremely well-drawn and Mr Growick, most importantly, does not falter with a very good ear for Holmesian dialogue indeed. Highly recommended. A five-star effort."
The Baker Street Society

Also published in Italian, Russian, and audio versions and the sequel 'The Revenge of Sherlock Holmes' is released in spring 2014.

www.mxpublishing.com

www.ingramcontent.com/pod-product-compliance
Lightning Source LLC
Chambersburg PA
CBHW080820020726
47501CB00009B/2357